A Safe Harbor

A bootlegger will save her life. A debutante will steal his heart.

Joan Fuller enjoyed a privileged life—until her wealth and connections garnered her the wrong sort of attention. Her rejection of a textile heir's proposal comes back to bite her when he turns out to be a werewolf on the prowl for a mate.

She may have been turned against her will, but now that she's part of his pack she sets out to protect all its women. Even if that means joining forces with a witch and a vampire—and leaving the comfort of Boston.

Former bootlegger Seamus Whelan has cleaned up his act, but when his old partner Gavin comes to him for help, he can't say no—no matter how deadly the threat. Escorting some female wolves to safety should have been easy, except their leader is a prim ex-debutante with enough power to challenge Seamus himself.

Her courage captures his interest, and her first hesitant kiss ensnares his heart. But before they can build a haven for their kind, they must free themselves of the past—and the powerful man who's out to teach her a lesson she may not survive...

Warning: This novella contains a rakish werewolf bootlegger forced to join forces with a teetotaling ex-debutante as they fight epic battles, engage in criminal activities and eventually give in to inappropriate passion on a kitchen counter.

Undertow

Being needed isn't half as desirable as being wanted.

Victor left behind a life of crime to focus on a new vision—helping his alpha build an island sanctuary for werewolves. Harsh experiences prepared him for the hardships involved, except when it comes to dealing with the young female refugees of the brutal Boston pack—especially Simone, who rouses his inner wolf like no other. A woman he must resist, or risk becoming just the latest man to make demands on her.

Born to wealth and privilege, Simone lost everything when she fell for the seductive whispers of the textile heir who turned her. Once adrift, now she is fired by a new sense of purpose—the chance to broker peace between werewolves and European wizards. Yet even as Europe beckons, her instincts—the same ones that led to trouble before—keep drawing her back to Victor.

During a sailing trip to the mainland for supplies, Victor finds it impossible to hold himself aloof from the warm, engaging Simone. And when a winter storm traps them together during a full moon, she breaks through his walls so easily and completely, the question is no longer how he'll stay away, but how he'll let her go.

Warning: This novella contains werewolves engaged in such improbable (but legal) activities as lobster fishing and sailing during nor'easters. The breaking and entering and instinct-driven sex on every surface in someone else's summer cottage is a little more criminal.

Look for these titles by
Moira Rogers

Now Available:

Southern Arcana Series
Crux
Crossroads
Deadlock
Cipher

Red Rock Pass Series
Cry Sanctuary
Sanctuary Lost
Sanctuary's Price
Sanctuary Unbound

Building Sanctuary Series
A Safe Harbor
Undertow

Bloodhound Series
Wilder's Mate

And the Beast Series
Sabine
Kisri

Print Book Collection
Sanctuary
Building Sanctuary

Building Sanctuary

Moira Rogers

SAMHAIN
PUBLISHING

Samhain Publishing, Ltd.
11821 Mason Montgomery Rd., 4B
Cincinnati, OH 45249
www.samhainpublishing.com

Building Sanctuary
Print ISBN: 978-1-60928-279-0
A Safe Harbor Copyright © 2011 by Moira Rogers
Undertow Copyright © 2011 by Moira Rogers

Editing by Anne Scott
Cover by Angie Waters

A Safe Harbor ISBN 978-1-60928-137-3
First Samhain Publishing, Ltd. electronic publication: July 2010
Undertow, ISBN 978-1-60928-216-5
First Samhain Publishing, Ltd. electronic publication: October 2010
First Samhain Publishing, Ltd. print publication: September 2011

Contents

A Safe Harbor

Dedication

This is dedicated to our intrepid editor, because she doesn't run screaming when we say things like, "We kind of want to write a historical, only with werewolves. Maybe set during the Great Depression." Instead, she says (and I paraphrase poorly, as she is much more eloquent than this), "Go for it!"

We also have to thank Grammy Rogers for her invaluable research help. No one knows Maine like Grammy.

Chapter One

"Doesn't look much like a vampire's lair." Victor's voice held a steely thread of tension.

And it was no wonder—the man loathed vampires as much as most wolves despised wizards. "This must be the place," Seamus told him. "Not another house for miles."

"How desperate would you have to be to leave a pack for this?"

"Fairly damn desperate." That easily described most people these days. Relief rolls were jam-packed and hundreds of thousands had taken to the roads, traveling in search of work. "Gavin didn't say what the circumstances were, but he did say he trusted the vampire. That's odd for him."

"Gavin Hamilton's always made odd friends." Victor's eyes narrowed as they neared the house. "The place is damn big. You sure we brought enough cars?"

Gavin's words came back to him. *You'll need three cars, maybe four. It's a fucking mess, Seamus. I—I can't explain right now.* "We'll muddle through."

"We always do."

"We're driving a handful of people, that's all. No cargo, no risk." A lie, and they both knew it.

The drive consisted of two dirt ruts worn through the grass, and Seamus navigated it slowly. "Maybe you should all wait for me out here. Less chance of trouble."

"Don't like the idea of you facing off with a vampire with no one at your back."

"Gavin didn't mention Adam Dubois being the problem here."

"Vampires are always the problem, when you get down to it." Victor turned, presenting a hard profile as he stared out the window at the untamed mess of a front yard. "But it ain't these girls' fault that no wolves stepped up to do their duty and protect them. I don't care how hard times are, every wolf in Boston deserves a thrashing."

"You'll get no argument from me." Seamus parked the car. "We'll soon see what's going on, though."

The porch steps creaked as he climbed them, and he bypassed the plain brass knocker in favor of pounding his fist on the door. Paint flaked off, and he watched it drift to the boards underfoot.

A woman opened the door, her skirt hiked halfway to her hips and blood drying into a sticky mess in her dark hair. She also had a rifle pointed at his chest.

Pulling his own piece seemed like a bad idea, so he murmured an apology, raised both hands and stepped back. "Hope I've got the right place. Gavin's expecting me."

Her gaze raked over him. She might be disheveled, but there was no mistaking the prissy superiority in her eyes as she tightened her grip on the weapon. "He said he was expecting a friend."

"Aye, that'd be me." He arched an eyebrow. "Is he around?"

"He's out back." The barrel of the rifle wavered and dipped toward the ground. "Are you Mr. Hamilton's business associate?"

The truth would horrify someone like her. For that reason

alone, he took great pleasure in giving it to her. "We used to run the streets together, back in the day."

Her lips pressed into a severe line, disapproval etched in every line of her stiff body. "Of course you did."

"Joan, if that's Whelan, let him in." The masculine voice drifted in from the other room, not Gavin's familiar brogue but a thick New England accent edged with dark power. *The vampire.* Joan's expression tightened, but she pivoted abruptly and stalked deeper into the farmhouse, clearly expecting him to follow.

"You boys stay on the porch," Seamus called back. His companions didn't need to be told again, but it might put the skittish woman more at ease. "I'll talk to Gavin, see what's what."

The house was dark, even in the afternoon sunlight, but it wasn't quiet. Soft moans of distress drifted down the halls and through the walls. Joan's footsteps thumped unevenly, and the scent of fresh, hot blood trailed after her. "You're hurt. Who else is?"

"I'm fine," she said, the words brittle enough to break. "There are twelve others. Seven are hurt, two badly."

"Wolves?"

"All of us. Except for Adam, obviously."

"When?"

The answer was too long coming, which meant she knew just how bad it sounded. "A few hours before dawn."

Unless she'd had her leg damn near ripped off, she should have been well on her way to fine already. "What in hell did you people tangle with?"

She turned again, holding her ground in spite of injury and obvious exhaustion. "What did Mr. Hamilton tell you?"

Not enough, not yet. "Where is he?"

Joan took a step back and nodded toward the door. "Out back. One of the new wolves panicked and can't shift back. I'm too drained to help her."

The back door hung slightly ajar, and Seamus pushed through it. He spotted Gavin immediately, a large gray wolf standing, alert, while a smaller wolf paced anxiously around him. He didn't yield, but he didn't push, either. As soon as Seamus stepped into the yard the female yipped and sidled away, darting to put the bulk of Gavin's body in front of her.

Fear hung in the air, thick enough to choke a human, and underneath it the smells of blood and lead and powder, evidence of a vicious battle. The wind shifted, bringing with it the whisper of shoes on the grass behind him—and the scent of the vampire.

He stepped up next to Seamus and watched Gavin begin the careful process of soothing the agitated wolf. "That's Ingrid. She's sixteen and three months changed."

Too young. Seamus could still remember the first few bewildering months after his own transformation. "And not by choice?"

"Choice." Adam made the word sound bitter. "She was a poor girl seduced into a life she couldn't understand. And after he'd had her enough times for the shine to wear off..."

No one who hadn't experienced the change *could* understand, and hearing the vampire speak as though he had the authority to do so raised Seamus's hackles. "Who are you to decide what people understand and what they don't?"

The vampire had a laugh like sandpaper against stone. "Didn't Hamilton tell you? I'm their alpha."

Seamus snorted and lit a cigarette. "He said something to that effect, but you don't smell like a wolf to me."

"Doesn't matter. What matters now is that these people

need to get to safety, and Gavin says you and your boys can make it happen."

He sounded defensive but worried. As quickly as that, Seamus's ire died. "We can. It depends, some."

"On?"

"On who you've got after you and your pack."

The vampire sighed, and Seamus knew he wouldn't like the answer. "Edwin Lancaster."

Even living under a rock wouldn't save a man from knowing the name. Wealthy and influential, both in human and wolf society, Edwin Lancaster was heir to a textile fortune...and a spoiled ass who got everything he wanted.

"What'd you—" He bit off the words with a curse, suddenly sure what Adam Dubois had done to anger Lancaster. "Who is it? The girl inside, the one with the limp?"

Adam didn't answer at first. He watched Gavin, who had gotten the anxious, confused wolf calmed enough to drop to the ground. Her small body trembled as a soft, tentative tendril of power uncurled, gentle enough to mark her as a weaker wolf.

At that first tug of magic, Adam and Seamus both turned their backs. "A lot of the women here are Lancaster's discarded playmates. He likes them young, impressionable and submissive."

It was the last way Seamus would have described the woman who'd stuck the business end of a rifle in his face. "If he tossed them, what does he care? You gather them up and...what? It makes him jealous?"

"I'm a vampire," Adam replied, his voice weary. "I'm told it's instinct. I suppose that's one of those things I won't ever understand."

"Also wrapped up in the fact that he's a self-centered asshole, I'm guessing." Seamus tossed his cigarette to the ground and stomped it out. "You don't throw away things you care about. And if you don't care about them, you don't deserve to have them."

He could feel the heavy weight of the man's blatant appraisal, but before he could respond a shaky female voice rose behind them. "A-Adam?"

Adam pulled his shirt over his head without hesitation. "It's okay, Ingrid. You're safe now."

Silence, except for the soft slide of fabric against skin and the girl's nervous, too-quick breaths. Then, "Are the others back?"

"Soon," Adam murmured. The girl seemed reassured, but Seamus could hear the lie.

Gavin stepped close and laid a hand on Seamus's shoulder. "Can we speak?"

They walked away from Dubois and the girl, and Seamus took a deep breath. "What was she talking about, Gavin? The others? Are there more wounded?"

He hesitated. "Captured."

"Shit." Seamus shoved both hands through his hair. "You're going after them."

"Yes, me and Adam."

"Don't you need me and the boys? We can find someone else to—"

"No." Gavin spoke sharply. "You take Joan and the others, and you get them to safety. They need a chance to heal."

"Why aren't they *now*?" Frustration colored his voice, but he couldn't help it. "What the fuck is going on?"

"Blood bonds," his oldest friend whispered hoarsely. "Adam has them, after a fashion, with all his followers. Some of them are in trouble, others need to get to safety, and you need to not ask so damn many questions."

He'd known Gavin Hamilton for years, had run with him in the streets of New York. Somehow, they'd avoided the gangs and the trouble that came with them, and always managed to stay a step ahead of whatever law they were breaking.

He trusted Gavin.

Seamus clapped a hand to his friend's back. "Tell me what I need to do."

There was no time for a proper bath, though the polished tub stood empty with its shiny new pipes gleaming and a freshly washed stack of towels beside it. For some of the girls, the ability to twist a knob and fill the tub with hot water had been a luxury more magical than the fact that they changed to wolves with every full moon.

Those were mostly Edwin's girls. Girls so poor they'd never known anything but heating pot after pot of water to fill a tub a bit at a time, if they were even that lucky. She had to credit the man with some cunning—he'd been very sure to pick girls unlikely to be missed. Orphans and farmers' daughters and maids who would be assumed to have abandoned their drudgery in favor of running off with a man. Oh yes, Edwin chose well.

Most of the time.

Joan sighed and did her best to ignore the tub as she stripped the torn, bloodstained dress from her body quickly but carefully. Even if there had been time to immerse herself in hot, clean water, she couldn't have. Simone had just changed the bandage wrapped around the wound on her calf, and it *still* hadn't healed. Instead Joan had stitches holding her skin together while sluggish power stirred inside her.

Not enough. Not nearly enough, and fear clawed inside her

as she tried not to imagine what it could mean. The bond with Adam would take what it needed to keep their people strong, but it had never drawn so much from her before, never felt like a noose around her neck. She was the most powerful wolf. Her magic fed the pack, fed *everyone*.

Including the wolves left to Edwin's surely untender mercies.

Every heartbeat increased her weariness, until exhaustion weighed so heavy that even simple chores seemed insurmountable obstacles. She fumbled with the knob for the hot water, then hesitated. Their supply wasn't endless, and it might be needed for more important things before the day was done. Gritting her teeth, she twisted on the cold water instead.

Autumn had come early to Massachusetts, and washing the blood from her hair wasn't as easy as she'd hoped. It had dried into a tacky, sticky mess, tangling around her fingers until she wanted to scream with frustration.

By the time the water ran clear, she was shivering in just her undergarments. She tucked one of the thick towels around her body and used another to rub at her hair, bracing herself for the fact she still had to wash her face, arms and neck in the icy water.

"You need some help."

Joan barely bit down in time to hold back a startled noise as she spun and found herself looking into gentle blue eyes. It was the new man, the one who'd come to speak to Adam's friend. Nothing should have made her so oblivious that she disregarded the sound of footsteps in the hallway, which meant she had left weary behind and careened into recklessly exhausted.

But not so exhausted as to tolerate a man staring at her with such blatant appraisal. She gripped the towel and tried to summon her fiercest glare as she pretended his words had been

18

a question instead of an arrogant, presumptuous statement. "I'm fine. Please close the door behind you."

"We're going to be working together." He stepped into the bathroom and, indeed, shut the door behind him. "That means we need to talk."

She'd seen women sporting dresses that bared more skin than her towel, but it didn't make her feel less naked. The press of his power didn't help—he was clearly a strong wolf, one full of rough, edgy dominance that stirred the wolf inside her with unrestrained curiosity.

She had to get rid of him. "I'll be out in a few minutes. If you or the men you brought need anything, you can ask Simone. She's in the kitchen."

"We had a lovely conversation." He smiled suddenly, not a grin or a smirk, and it transformed his face from hard to boyishly handsome. "She told me to come talk to you."

Of course she had. Humans might judge authority by gender or age or social standing or money, but wolves only cared for power. It didn't matter that she was twenty-four and female, that she'd lost her inheritance and any hope of being accepted or respected by polite society. She had raw power, so she was in charge.

The heaviness of her responsibility settled over her. Soon she'd slide to the floor under the weight of it, crushed beyond repair.

His smile slipped away. "Are you ill?"

"No." She didn't have the luxury of giving up, not until they were safe. And if the man refused to leave, she'd just wash in front of him. Modesty seemed foolish when they could all be dead before seeing another dawn.

So she turned on the water again, just enough to wet a washcloth, then set to work on the blood smeared on her forearm. "I don't believe Mr. Hamilton told me your name."

"Seamus." She could see him in the mirror, his brown hair falling over his forehead as he leaned against the wall. "Gavin told me there's some sort of spell draining magic and keeping the wolves here from healing. You said earlier some are hurt worse than you?"

"A few. Mostly the men." And though both of the survivors had fought hard, they'd been weaker wolves. Wolves who had come to Adam afraid they wouldn't be able to protect their mates from the roving eyes and covetous urges of the Boston alpha and his inner circle. Adam had given them safety...for a time. "The attackers weren't trying to kill the women, just capture them."

If it shocked him, he didn't show it. "Everyone has to be moved. We're loading up in cars and heading closer to the coast."

"To hide." She rinsed the washcloth and stepped closer to the mirror to wipe away the blood streaking her face. There were scratches too, and at least one shallow cut on her shoulder that had healed to a thin pink line. "Adam's trying to break the bonds we have with him. As soon as he figures out how, the others should begin healing again."

"Not a moment too soon."

No. Probably too late, but Astrid had cast the spells, and without her, Adam struggled against a lack of knowledge and a deficit of power. "He's doing his best. We all are."

"I don't doubt that." Seamus stepped toward her. "Now it's partly my responsibility too."

The bathroom was too small to make the press of his power anything but too intimate, especially in her current state of undress. She met his gaze in the mirror and put the punch of her remaining energy into it. "How much have Adam and Mr. Hamilton explained to you?"

20

"Enough." He reached over her shoulder. "Let me."

"No!" The word escaped on a surge of panic, and exhaustion had clearly made a fool of her because she didn't realize he wasn't reaching for the towel or her body until his fingers closed around the washcloth.

She closed her eyes so she wouldn't have to see his face in the mirror as she let him take the cloth. "As you might imagine, we're all unusually high strung."

"I'm sorry. I thought I was being careful." The water ran, and he sighed. "I'm sorry."

"It's all right." Joan drew in a steadying breath and wished she hadn't. With him so close, his scent overwhelmed everything. It was masculine, uncompromising, smells she associated with the type of men she'd never had much to do with before Adam. Sweat and dirt and liquor and the lead and gunpowder that meant he had a weapon on him, and underneath all that the indefinable *something* that said wolf.

Or maybe that wasn't a scent at all, but the brush of magic. It was more primal than smell, an instinctive prompting that told her another wolf was near. And more than that—a strong wolf. A male. An alpha, dominant whether he led a pack or not, a wolf she didn't have to protect. Someone who could help her protect those in her care.

Or someone who could hurt you. The voice of experience, not instinct, but a valid concern and one he'd have to be well prepared to deal with if he planned to help them. "My people will be nervous around you, and it can't be helped. No wolf looks to a witch and vampire for protection if she's known kindness from her alphas."

Again, he didn't seem surprised. "Indeed." He eased the cloth over the back of her neck. "You got clawed back here, but it's mostly healed."

Memories of the frantic, vicious fight threatened to surface,

21

and she shoved them back ruthlessly. "They weren't going to kill me. I rather imagine they were all under very strict orders to ensure they didn't, in fact."

"Because of Lancaster."

If only Edwin Lancaster were their sole concern. "He's not happy with me, but it's worse than that. I defied the Boston alpha."

His touch faltered for a moment. "Jesus Christ."

Yes, Seamus would understand what that meant in a way Adam never could. She opened her eyes and met his gaze in the mirror. "I did what I had to. I couldn't watch them suffer."

He watched her in the mirror, his expression thoughtful. "I can handle getting your people to safety, but I'll need your help."

"*My* help?" She turned and stared at him as anger bubbled up. "They're my people. I will give everything for them, up to and including my life. But I'll appreciate *your* help."

"Calm down, Joan. I know this is your burden." His voice gentled. "Let me take it, just for a little while."

If she gave him an inch there'd be nothing left of her. "Men don't take power for a little while."

After a moment, he nodded and draped the bloodstained cloth over the edge of the sink. "I'll wait downstairs."

Every instinct inside her screamed in warning, and she thought it was the wolf clamoring for her to apologize, to do anything to keep Seamus from leaving and taking that aura of strength and safety with him.

She turned, braced to ignore her wolf's angry demands, but what splintered through her was pain, blinding physical agony so sharp she screamed before she could stop herself. Digging her teeth into her lower lip didn't help because she wasn't the only one screaming, and the screams from the rest of the house were high and pained and so *afraid...*

Joan didn't realize her knees had given out until strong arms locked around her waist. Pain made the room swim, but she held back another cry of pain, locked it inside until her voice only trembled a little. "Adam. I need to get to Adam."

Seamus had already slipped one arm under her knees. He lifted her with ease and shouldered through the bathroom door. "Just hang on, Joan. You'll be all right."

How could she tell him she wasn't afraid for herself? She had felt pain through the bonds before, the agony of someone connected to them dying a hard death. But it had been over in a heartbeat. It hadn't twisted inside her until the world constricted to nothing but agony.

Somewhere out there, one of her people was dying. Slowly.

Chapter Two

The situation had taken an even sharper turn for the worse than Seamus expected. He leaned against the parlor wall beside Gavin and watched as Adam clutched at Joan's arm until she'd surely bear bruises in the shape of his hand.

Joan seemed oblivious, at least to his grip. Steely, unwavering stubbornness filled her hazel eyes as she stared up at the vampire. "Do it."

Adam shook his head. "You're hurt. You're not strong enough."

"I'm always strong enough. Do it."

Uneasy, Seamus glanced at Gavin. His friend raised one shoulder in a shrug.

Adam closed his eyes, and Joan swayed on her knees as the flickering strength inside her flared. Magic twisted in the room, prickling over Seamus's skin, and he swore he *saw* it as power flowed from Joan to Adam. She seemed to wilt as he grew stronger, pulsing with energy that tasted more like a wolf than a vampire.

Silence stretched between them for ten of Joan's too-quick heartbeats, and Adam swore. "I found them. They're far, probably fifty miles northwest. It's Opal. They're hurting her." Frustration and rage colored his voice.

Joan, by contrast, sounded calm. Almost numb. "Cut her

loose."

"*No.*"

Power pulsed, and a hoarse, gasping sob echoed down the hallway. Pain etched lines in Joan's face, and Seamus saw tears in her eyes before she squeezed them shut. "Cut her loose, Adam. She's drawing too much power."

"She'll *die* without it."

"The rest of us will die if you don't."

They were talking about the bonds. Seamus's blood chilled, and he stood straighter as Adam snarled. The vampire's fingers tightened around Joan's arm until she hissed in a pained breath, but he released her a heartbeat later.

The whimpers and sobs from upstairs cut off abruptly. Adam slumped forward, and Joan braced both hands on his shoulders. "Don't stop. Use my power to release the people here. You can feed if you need to."

Adam knocked her hands away. "I'm not taking anything else from you. I'm not helping you commit slow suicide."

Gavin stepped forward, but Seamus held out an arm to stop him. "You're running into a fight, Hamilton. I'm running *from* one."

"Seamus—"

He ignored Gavin. "I'll do it."

Joan inched back, making room in front of Adam. Someone had wrapped a blanket around her when they'd arrived in the parlor, but the fabric had slipped to her waist. She eased it back up around her shoulders, her fingers trembling, and spoke as Seamus knelt beside her. "Thank you."

Looking at her, weak and injured, stirred a dangerous, protective rage. Even darker was the possessiveness her wide, grateful gaze elicited. "You're welcome."

"Have you ever had a vampire feed from you before?" Adam asked.

Seamus couldn't tear his gaze away from Joan's. "No."

Joan wet her lips and spoke without looking away. "His forearm, Adam. He'll be like me. Not very comfortable with the idea of a strange man marking his neck."

The thought of Adam Dubois marking her *anywhere* drew a growl from Seamus's throat. "Do whatever you need to do."

"His forearm," Joan repeated, and this time it was an order. She scooted closer, until her blanket-covered knees brushed his, and reached out to touch his hand. "Vampires don't gain power from the quantity of blood. It's the quality—the willingness of the gift or the emotional charge behind it. If you're uncomfortable or fighting him, even instinctively, it will take more."

Which told him nothing about how to handle it. "Don't think I can avoid being uncomfortable. How do I do this?"

Joan shifted her gaze over his shoulder, to where Adam had to be. She didn't say anything, but her lips pressed together and a slow, pink flush rose in her cheeks. When she looked back at Seamus, self-consciousness and an odd anticipation clashed in her eyes. "Hold out your arm."

His shirtsleeve was half-rolled anyway, so he tugged it up and stretched out his arm. Joan lifted her hand and pushed it up another few inches, her fingertips brushing his skin in tiny, glancing touches that awakened his body.

When she had his sleeve arranged to her satisfaction, she moved her hand to his shoulder. "Watch me," she whispered as Adam's fingers closed around his wrist. "If your wolf needs distraction, use me."

Any more distraction, and he'd have to chase her through the backyard and take her where he caught her. Fiery pain shot up his arm as Adam's teeth closed on his skin, but he stood his ground, determined not to let anyone, least of all Joan, see his discomfort. "I'm plenty tough, honey."

The worry didn't fade from her eyes. She lifted her hand to his cheek, her touch feather-light. "It shouldn't take long. If he has enough power he can concentrate and break the bonds one at a time instead of just severing them all. He needs to stay connected to the ones who've been captured so he can use that to find them."

"Right." Seamus forced himself to breathe. He understood what Adam needed to do, but that didn't help the trapped feeling. The wolf inside him had been bitten, subdued, and he didn't like it. "Damn it all."

"Shh." Small, delicate fingers curled around the back of his neck, and she leaned in until a hairsbreadth separated their mouths. "He won't hurt you. Can't dominate you. You're giving a gift."

Now that she'd cleaned away the blood, he could smell her under the soap. Her skin was smooth and pale, her hair shiny and curling the tiniest bit as it dried. He wanted to kiss her, so he held himself still. "I can't—"

Her lips touched his. Soft, so soft it was hardly a kiss. It could have been an accident, considering how quickly she pulled away, but a moment later she was back again, her head tilted and her lips pressing more firmly, albeit off-center.

She didn't know how to kiss, but she tasted as good as she smelled. He opened his mouth a little, just to see if she'd deepen the gentle caress. Tension trembled in her body, but she parted her lips as if following his lead.

The burn of panic subsided, replaced by an entirely different kind of heat. Seamus tore his mouth from hers and gritted his teeth again. "How much longer?"

"Not much," she whispered, her voice shaking with

27

helplessness. "I'd do it if I could. I'm sorry."

It was far from a mere apology or excuse. She meant the words with an intensity that drew him, until all he could think of was kissing her again. Her mouth was pliant under his, willing, though she clearly had no idea what to do.

He stroked his thumb over the curve of her cheek. She made a quiet noise that turned into a gasp as he traced his tongue over her lips. Magic flared between them, power tinged with feral need.

She needed this.

He slid his fingers into her dark hair, and the cool, damp strands clung to his skin. "Joan."

A soft, hungry growl tickled his ears. Her nails pricked the back of his neck. The tip of her tongue darted out, dragged along his lip as if she was tasting him.

The pain vanished, though it took his addled mind a few seconds to register that fact. Seamus lifted his head and found Adam watching them, gaze slightly unfocused. "It's over, Joan."

She started at the sound of Adam's voice and jerked back, scrambling to pull the blanket tight around her shoulders. The flush in her cheeks deepened from pink to red as she tugged at the cloth until it covered everything up to and including her chin. "Is it enough?"

"It's enough," Adam replied without looking away from Seamus. "Gavin, can you go upstairs to the room where the injured are and make sure they all stay calm? This may disorient some of them."

"Got it." Gavin took off down the hall.

Seamus watched absently as the holes in his inner arm closed. "Is there anything else I can do?"

"Joan." It sounded like the answer to his question until Adam knelt in front of the young woman. He reached out and touched her cheek, and a tired smile curved his lips. "I'm sorry, sweetheart. It's going to hurt. You were the first."

Joan didn't flinch. "I know."

Adam rocked to his feet. "Watch her."

It was going to hurt her, and Seamus wanted to take her away, protect her from it. His hands shook, and he closed them into fists.

Whatever the vampire was doing, it was subtle—at first. Aside from a faint stirring of energy, Adam could have been sitting quietly, staring at nothing. The first real indication of something happening was Joan's tiny, pained gasp. Her body went stiff, and magic lashed through the room, rising ferociously as one piercing, heartbreaking scream tore free of her throat.

In the next moment, she went wild. Everything human faded from her eyes as she jumped to her feet, deadly graceful and inhumanly fast. She clawed at her undergarments, tearing her panties and bra. Most of the fabric fell to the floor, but Adam didn't notice. He was intent on something else, something Seamus could neither see nor sense.

"Joan?" Seamus held out a hand. "Joan, honey, calm down."

A snarl was the only response he got before she hit the floor on her knees, fur already flowing over her body. She changed too fast, the magic ripping her apart, and the small brown wolf who took her place howled once in outraged pain before bolting for the back door.

"*Shit.*" Adam didn't move, and there was no one else. Seamus tugged off his boots and ripped at his vest and shirt. He had to chase her down, *calm* her down...and bring her back.

Someone had closed the door, a small mercy. It gave him time to tear at his pants as the rhythmic *thud* of Joan throwing herself against the door drifted in from the kitchen. Something crashed to the floor as he dropped his pants, dishes followed by the metallic clink of silverware. Then glass shattered.

He stalked through the house, tossing aside the rest of his clothes. By the time he opened the back door, he saw her, streaking across the lawn at full speed.

"God damn it." It took him a moment to call the spark of magic inside him. When he had it, the change flowed over him, easy and familiar.

He ran after her.

Joan would have stopped running before she hit the edge of the clearing if Seamus hadn't chased her.

Her paws dug deep into the dirt as she bolted between two trees. Pain had forced her to run, but it was her wolf who made her continue. With the sun hanging low in the west the woods would be dark, and she knew them intimately. Seamus would have to work to catch her...and she wanted him to work.

He yipped and snarled but kept pace with her despite his disadvantage, the sounds growing closer as he gained. Her wolf was ready to be caught, but Joan had reclaimed just enough sense to know what often followed a challenge and a chase between male and female wolves.

Nerves gave her speed. She darted between two bushes and leapt over a fallen log, but her paws slipped on the damp leaves on the opposite side.

Seamus didn't stumble. He sailed past her, large but fast, and rounded, cutting her off.

With her path blocked, Joan panted for breath and studied her adversary. The black wolf in front of her outweighed her by a fair margin and seemed more intimidating than his human counterpart. As loudly as her wolf had clamored before, now she'd fallen suspiciously silent.

He sat and watched her, tensed and poised to move again. Backing down would bring the confrontation to an end, but she'd never submitted to anyone in her short existence as a werewolf. So she bared her teeth and lunged to the side, ready to slide to the ground and twist out of the way if he pounced.

He matched her movements, close enough to block but not crowd her. She snarled and dodged the opposite way, but he moved just as fast, cutting off her escape.

Joan was preparing to turn and charge back the way she'd come when the pain hit her, twice as hard as the wave of agony that had caused her to shift and riding on a swell of power so intense it stole her breath. Her legs collapsed, spilling her onto the damp leaves as magic tore through her. She didn't realize she'd shifted again until she heard her own pained whimpers, and even that didn't matter when the bonds tying her to Adam and the rest of her people finally snapped.

Nothing had ever felt so wrong. The pain ceased almost at once but left behind a gaping hole, abject emptiness in the place that had held life and a subtle awareness of the wolves tied to her. She choked on a sob and dug her fingers into the dirt, grasping for something, *anything* to take the place of what she'd lost.

"Shh. I've got you." Gentle hands skimmed her back, grasped her shoulders. "I've got you."

"I can't—" The air burned as she gasped in a breath. It was too cold to be naked on the forest floor, and numbness followed pain. "I can't feel anything."

Seamus rubbed a hand over her leg, carefully skirting her wound. "Whatever he did worked. You tore your stitches, but you're healing."

He didn't understand. Joan clutched at the leaves and dirt as her eyes burned with tears she refused to shed. "I can't feel *anything.*"

"The broken bonds?" His hand stroked her skin again. "It's for the best, Joan. It's like you told Dubois."

"I have to go back." Pain shredded through her as she pushed to her knees. "We have to leave."

"Joan." He watched her with knowing blue eyes. "You did the right thing."

Her own words drifted up. *You have to cut her loose.* Opal was probably dead now—a quick, merciful death instead of one prolonged by energy that wasn't her own. It was too easy to call to mind the girl's round, cheerful face and her bright green eyes. Nineteen years old and in love with life, if a little too fond of men for her own good.

And now she was dead.

If Joan thought about it, she'd scream until her throat bled. "I need to change back. I can't run fast enough like this."

Seamus released her and moved back. "Take it slow."

She didn't have a choice. That spark of magic inside was barely a flicker, and no matter how many times she grasped for it, the change eluded her. Tiny discomforts began to intrude— the knowledge that she was naked in front of a man, that the ground was cold and her body had begun to shake. Each one made it harder to concentrate until tears flowed and her fingers scraped helplessly against the ground.

In the end, she could only climb to her feet and ignore the biting chill of the wind against bare skin as she started back toward the farmhouse on unsteady human legs.

Magic flared behind her, and Seamus trotted past her, once again wearing his wolf form. He didn't look back, and he didn't run ahead. Instead he gave her company without sacrificing the tiny shreds of her dignity, and through the pain and the weariness, something warm unfurled in her chest. Gratitude, or even hope.

An impossibly long road lay ahead of her, too many challenges before she'd know she'd found sanctuary for the people in her care. But maybe—*maybe*—she didn't have to do it alone.

Seamus tucked one last duffel into the trunk of his car and glanced at Adam and Gavin. "This it?"

Adam nodded, but his gaze was fixed on the window. In the encroaching darkness it was hard to make out the outline of all the people squeezed into the back of the car, but Joan's profile was clear. Her hand stroked soothingly over the hair of the woman next to her, a pregnant young wolf fairly trembling with nerves.

The wolves had grown stronger, but Adam's presence seemed to be fading. Seamus could hardly sense any magic at all as the vampire turned his back on the car, his expression bleak. "Help her. She's strong, but she's so damn *young.*"

There was no reason to argue. "They all are."

"I know." Adam's voice dropped to a rumbling whisper. "If you hurt her, I'll find you and tear you apart."

It was to be expected, the warning before Seamus drove off with a handful of Adam's charges. That the vampire would focus on warning him off Joan made sense. "I don't plan to hurt anyone, and that's the best you're going to get."

Oddly, Adam smiled. "That's all I want. Joan doesn't need me to drive away romantic suitors. I could never do it as ruthlessly as she does. Stay in the caves until nightfall tomorrow. If Gavin and I don't show up by then..."

"We'll head straight for Philadelphia," Seamus reassured him. "Though I'd rather you didn't get my friend killed."

33

"I'll do my best not to." Adam pivoted and strode along the side of the car to tap softly on the window next to Joan's head. She rolled it down, and their soft whispers drifted back to Seamus's ears.

"Got everything?" Gavin asked him, drowning out the low, tired sound of Joan's voice.

"I think so. Shouldn't take us long to reach the caves, and we have the supplies we need." Food, water...and weapons. Just in case.

Gavin clapped a hand to his shoulder. "Be careful."

"*You* be careful, old man." It was an old joke that had found its genesis in their younger years, when no one had believed Seamus was five years Gavin's senior. "Crazed alpha wolves and vampires?"

"We'll be fine." His friend's smile was steady, even. It belied the angry roil of power beneath his calm facade.

Seamus punched him on the shoulder. "Give 'em hell."

The soft slam of a car door cut through the silence. Seamus followed the noise and found Joan ushering a curvy little blonde and a thin, tired-looking man into the backseat. They squeezed in somehow, but it left Joan with nowhere to sit. She closed the door and met Seamus's eyes for the briefest second before circling the car to the front passenger side.

Seamus nodded to Adam as he moved to the driver's door. "Remember what I said."

Adam patted the top of the car. "We'll see you tomorrow night."

Seamus climbed behind the wheel. "Everybody settled?"

Joan sat in the middle of the bench seat, a sleepy young woman leaning against her right side. After slipping an arm around her companion, Joan glanced at the wolves in the backseat. "I think we're ready."

Seamus turned the key in the starter, and the engine rumbled to life. "We'll be on the road for a couple of hours. Everybody just speak up if you need to stop."

No one replied, not even Joan, whose arm brushed his as she arranged the already dozing woman more comfortably against her shoulder.

They all seemed drained. He made it no more than five miles before the first quiet snore rose in the back of the car. The tense press of magic began to ease over the next few miles, until even the men had calmed somewhat.

Only Joan refused to relax. She sat stiffly next to him, her body held carefully, as if to keep all contact to an absolute minimum. As the moon brightened, he noted that a gentle blush crept up her cheeks every time she accidentally touched him.

"Forget about the kiss," he urged her quietly. "You were helping me, that's all. I don't expect—well. I understand."

It shouldn't have been possible for her to stiffen further, but she made a good attempt. "I'd already forgotten. It was hardly memorable, was it?"

It was too defensive to be an honest reaction. "You'll have to forgive me, darling. I wasn't at my best."

"If you say so." She kept her voice as soft as his, and no one in the back moved or made a sound. Judging by the steady, even breaths, he and Joan were the only ones awake—or the only ones willing to acknowledge they were.

The question needed answering. "What have you all been doing with yourselves out here? Hiding away from the world?"

"Hiding away from other werewolves," she countered. "Most of the people here weren't safe in the Boston pack."

"But they were safe with Dubois?"

"Don't be insulting."

Seamus sighed. "I'm not being insulting, lady. I'm asking."

"We weren't just safe. We were happy." She shifted positions, clearly restless, and the movement pressed her hip against his. This time she didn't jerk away, though she didn't move closer, either. "There were some...unusual arrangements between some of the men and women, but no one did anything he or she didn't want."

"Unusual arrangements?" He fought a smile.

The color was back in her cheeks, brighter than ever. "Nothing as unusual as the gossips would have you believe. I've heard some of the rumors. They're absurd."

"Are they?" He would never let on that he'd heard them, not to her. "Do I want to know?"

Joan stared straight ahead. "I suppose that depends on what sort of man you are."

She'd already convinced herself he was the worst sort, and there would be no changing her mind. "Relax. I don't listen to idle gossip."

It seemed to relax her a little. "Thank you. The girls are..." Her voice dropped, barely a whisper. "Before they came here, many were coerced into indiscretions. Some were even forced. It's hard to listen to callous judgment of them, knowing what I do of their former situations."

"I also don't judge women for surviving."

"Then you're a rare man."

"Maybe I am." He didn't really think he was, but the belief had obviously made it easy for her to fall into Dubois' arms.

A distressed whimper pierced the tense silence, and Joan turned away to soothe the girl beside her with quiet murmurs and a gentle rush of power.

It didn't matter how young Joan was; even the older girls looked to her for guidance. "If anyone needs anything, you'll have to let me know. I doubt they'll tell me themselves."

"Probably not. It's not personal. It's just..." She trailed into uncomfortable silence, then sighed. "Adam only told me you're a friend of Gavin's, and Gavin is a friend of his. I don't know anything about you, or what you know about the Boston pack and how things are there."

And there was no way to put her at ease with the truth. "I tend to stay clear of Boston these days."

She tilted her head to study him, the weight of her gaze tangible. "Trouble with the pack?"

"Trouble with the law."

"Caves." It was barely a whisper, and more a thought given voice than a question. "Of course. I'm quite a little fool, aren't I?"

"How's that?"

That cool, disapproving tone was back. "It explains why Adam always had the very best liquor at his disposal. One of his more prominent vices."

Seamus grinned. "And you don't approve of drink, I gather."

"Not particularly. It turns men into fools and werewolves into animals."

He'd always been of the opinion that lack of self-control did both. "I see."

She slanted another of those long, searching looks at him. "I don't mean to be ungrateful," she said finally, the words almost tentative. "I appreciate your help, and the help of your associates. I don't need to approve of your...career."

"You certainly don't," he agreed. "I hate to disappoint a lady, the truth is that Gavin and I *used* to be involved in such activities. Not anymore."

"So what do you do now?" She sounded honestly curious.

"This and that. Investing, mostly. I didn't lose much when the market went belly-up."

"Then you're fortunate. I heard my family lost everything."

But she didn't *know*. He filed that away. "How did you wind up with Adam?"

"One of the wolves from Boston. She had a—a friend. A witch. The witch knew Adam." Her crisp, proper words had begun to slur a little, fatigue softening her voice and lending it a husky undertone. "Maggie had it hard in the pack, and I had...troubles. A lot of us did."

She was so exhausted she was about to fall asleep. "So you left them behind and made your own way."

"Mmm. Astrid had a plan. Astrid's our witch." Her head tilted to the side, bit by bit, until her temple rested atop the girl's head. It was a vulnerable position, one that left the smooth column of her neck bared to him, her throat unprotected.

Her skin looked pale, soft. The urge to taste her took him by surprise, and he dragged his gaze back to the winding road in front of the car. "Rest, Joan."

"It's okay. I'm awake."

He swallowed a chuckle. "You're sleeping."

"I'm tired." It escaped as a whisper, a confession. "I'm so very, very tired."

She could have been speaking of her physical exhaustion, but Seamus doubted it. Not with those shadows darkening her eyes as much as the hollows beneath them. He tightened his hands around the steering wheel. "I know, honey. I told you. I'll help."

She didn't reply, but she didn't need to. Her breathing evened out and the last of her restless power settled as she fell asleep. She either trusted him, at least a little, or she was too damn exhausted to care.

As much as he wished for the former, he'd bet on the latter.

Chapter Three

Something about the vastness of the ocean had the power to heal.

Joan cradled a battered tin cup in her hands more for the lingering heat than out of any desire to taste its contents. It barely qualified as coffee, though she couldn't complain. Having coffee at all was something of a miracle, considering the rugged conditions in which they'd found themselves.

The wind whipped over the water, bringing with it a sharp bite and the overpowering scent of brine. Everything smelled different this far from civilization. Sharper. Cleaner.

Wilder.

"It's beautiful, especially at night." Simone's lilting voice drifted from behind her, carried on the breeze. "Nothing like the city."

"No, I suppose it isn't." Joan turned and studied her friend in the glowing moonlight. "Is there trouble?"

"No, not at all." Simone dropped to the sand beside her, looking more like a tomboy than the once-celebrated debutante Joan knew her to be. "Everyone is settling in. Your friend has stocked the caves well. We shouldn't want for anything, except perhaps a bath."

They had almost a day before they could expect to hear from Adam or Gavin. Endless hours of tense, unsettled waiting.

"What about the men? No challenges?"

A hint of color crept over Simone's pale cheeks, and she shook her head. "It's been very calm. Quiet."

Joan was hardly in a position to ask probing questions, not when she'd fled the confines of the cave to escape the electric shock of magic that trembled through her every time Seamus stood too close. "Quiet is good, I suppose. Everyone needs their rest."

"Mmm." Simone hunched down into the blanket wrapped around her shoulders. "It's chilly. Do you want to share this?"

It made her smile. "Of course. Scoot on over."

The blanket was large and coarsely woven, and Simone settled it around both of them. "How long until we hear from Adam?"

In her darkest moments, Joan thought they never would. It was suicide, sending two men into the midst of the Boston pack, but it would have been even more reckless to drag a group of timid, traumatized subordinate wolves with them.

If it had been anyone else, Joan would have come up with a soothing lie, but Simone was the closest thing she had to a contemporary, a confidante, now. "I don't know. If we don't hear anything by tomorrow night, we're going south. Far enough to find someplace safe to go to ground."

The girl nodded. "Seems like they've got it all planned out."

"For now." Until they ended up in a strange city with no friends and hardly any resources. The small stash of cash she had on hand would secure them food and shelter for a month or two, but not even the tiny hoard of gold or the depressingly meager stack of mature bonds hidden away in her suitcase would sustain them for long. They had too many mouths to feed in a time when so many were already going hungry...

If she thought about it too much she'd scream, and it

wasn't even the most immediate problem. She'd seen the wariness in Seamus's eyes as he set his men to guard the perimeter. He didn't believe they'd escaped cleanly any more than Joan did, and that, at least, was a consolation. The criminal element might make her uncomfortable, but if anyone could keep them hidden, it would be men whose lives consisted of hiding.

Simone grasped her hand. "It will be fine, Joan. It will."

Strong as she was, even Simone needed reassurance. Joan forced a smile and curled her fingers tight around her friend's hand. "I know it will. It's just been a long few days, hasn't it?"

The redhead turned her face toward the sea. "With everything that's happened, even before the attack, that is one way to put it."

Joan judged a change in subject would do them both good. "How's Elise? Did they manage to make her comfortable?"

"I don't think anything short of delivering the baby is going to help at this point."

Another worry to add to the considerable list. Joan felt the weight pressing on her more acutely than ever, and this time not even the soothing repetition of waves lapping against the shore could still the panic in her heart. "We'll deal with that when we have to. How closely did you pay attention when Mary had her son?"

A hint of Simone's normally cheerful smile curved her lips. "Closely enough to know the process mostly takes care of itself."

The girl's unfailing optimism was simultaneously exhausting and endearing. This time Joan didn't have to struggle so hard to find an answering smile. "Well, then, I suppose there are some advantages to being werewolves. You'll keep an eye on her for me, won't you?"

"Of course I will. Will you—"

The crunch of boots on the rocks behind them interrupted Simone's words. Seamus stood there, his hands in his pockets. "I don't mean to intrude."

Joan hadn't sensed his approach, which signified either a frightening level of inattention or something more insidious— the possibility that her wolf had already judged him as safe as Simone. "You're not intruding. Is something the matter?"

"No, I..." He cleared his throat. "Just wanted to make sure you were doing all right."

Simone slid out from under the blanket and rose. "I'll check on Elise."

Traitor. Hard as she tried, Joan couldn't catch Simone's eyes before she made her escape, leaving Joan alone with a handsome werewolf and fiercely embarrassed that her own thoughts betrayed her by affording him such a telling adjective.

There were plenty more where that came from. Strong. Dangerous. Enticing. The silvery light of the moon slanted across the strong lines of Seamus's face, giving him a rakish look. Turning him into the sort of darkly romantic hero that would likely have all the girls aflutter.

As if she wasn't one of them. The animal inside stirred, filling her with a fierce, uncontrollable yearning. She had to avert her gaze, and even that wasn't enough to completely eliminate the husky undertone when she spoke. "I just needed a few moments to collect my thoughts."

"Would you like me to go?" he rasped.

She told him the truth because she didn't know what else to do. "I don't know. Would you like to stay?"

He didn't answer right away. He nudged at the rocks underfoot with his boot. "Are you holding it together?"

"I'm not screaming." Yet. And that was the seductive danger of his presence. It had been so much easier to hold things together when she knew she had no choice. The wind picked up again, slicing under her blanket and cutting through the bulky layers of her clothing until she shivered and gripped the blanket tighter. "I want to, though."

"We could run for a while."

Yes yes yes. Her wolf, and more a feeling than an actual thought, but she pushed it back ruthlessly. "I shouldn't. I need to stay close."

"Ah." Seamus squinted at her. "Victor can handle things for a while. And your friend—what's her name?"

"Simone." Who had blushed when mentioning Seamus's men. "I know it may seem foolish to you, but I'd feel better if I was nearby."

"Not foolish," he countered. "If that's what you want."

"Foolish because that's not what I want." Bitterness welled up inside her, and she closed her eyes as the words spilled out, low and laced with her guilt and shame. "I've put on a magnificent act, don't you think? Fooled everyone into believing I'm a leader? All I want to do is run away."

His hand fell to her shoulder, heavy and solid. "If you didn't want to run, I'd think you were touched in the head. You're *not* running, and that's the trick. Staying to lead even when you want to hide away."

"Is that it?" He was so warm, and her wolf wouldn't be denied that comfort, not if they were trapped in human form and bound to stay close to their people. Her arm crept out without permission, holding the blanket open in shy invitation. "Would you like to sit?"

He sat. After a slight hesitation, he pulled the blanket around his body. "Thank you, Joan."

"You're welcome." He was warm...but he wasn't touching her. Mere inches felt like a boundless chasm she could never cross, even if she desperately wanted to. It wasn't what she'd expected at all, not from the man who'd had no problem taking her mouth while others watched.

Of course, she could hardly be surprised he wasn't interested in doing so again. She didn't know how to kiss, and a man like him wouldn't have missed such a detail. In her ignorance, she'd proved herself every bit the frigid, prudish spinster Edwin had once sworn she'd become.

Seamus watched her, his gaze an almost tangible weight. "I know this must seem like cold comfort, but you're doing well."

It seemed a tiny bit condescending, but for all she knew he was twice or even thrice her age. Picking a fight with the only ally she had seemed petty and childish, so she accepted the words as she imagined he meant them. "Thank you. This...is not the life I expected to lead."

"Does anyone?" He blew out a breath. "I'm upsetting you."

"A little." She looked away, back out toward the ocean with its dark, frothy waves and untamed expanses. "But it isn't personal. Being upset with you is easier than thinking about the choices I've made."

He laughed softly, though the sound held no mirth. "Be as angry with me as you want, then. As long as it serves a useful purpose, I can take it."

"Are you sure? I'm told I'm impossibly tedious when I'm whipped into a frenzy of moral outrage."

"Nothing about you is tedious."

Her kiss certainly had been. She'd agonized over it plenty in the intervening time, fighting to convince herself she'd made a logical decision for the good of her people. Embarrassment made it easier to rationalize—obviously she'd been sacrificing herself for the greater good. If she'd truly wanted to kiss him, she wouldn't have done such a terrible job.

It amused her that she could still cling to pride when she had nothing else. Or maybe that was why she clung so fiercely, as if she could rewrite history if she replayed the events enough times in her head.

A pointless diversion. She'd kissed him.

She'd wanted to.

She *still* wanted to, and it had nothing to do with saving her people or herself. Even now just turning to look at him stoked that hunger, primal and oddly confident considering her sad lack of experience.

Something dark flashed in his eyes, and Seamus lifted one warm hand to her cheek. "You're looking at me like you want me to kiss you."

"Am I?" The words came out sounding breathless and foolish. Hungry, and she *was*—so, so hungry for his touch. Enough that she leaned into his hand to feel the rough texture of his fingers against her cheek.

"You are." He bent his head closer to hers. "Do you?"

Years of self-denial stretched out behind her, and her future held the same grim certainty. Inside, her wolf whined in protest, and for the first time in her life Joan didn't fight it. Here under the stars, with the ocean as her only witness, she could have one moment of selfishness.

So she didn't answer in words. Perhaps her clumsy kiss would inspire as little interest this time as it had last time, but she'd know she'd had the courage to try. She closed her eyes and found his lips with her own, savored the soft warmth that filled her at even the gentlest contact.

But it didn't stay gentle. Seamus groaned, pulled her closer and licked her mouth. "Let me in, Joan."

It became impossible to separate the gentle noise of waves breaking on the sand from the roaring in her ears. She grasped his shoulder, twisted her fingers in his vest as she let her head fall back. "I don't know what to do. Tell me."

"Open." His thumb brushed her lips and applied the barest pressure to her chin. "Open your mouth."

She did, and moaned when his tongue swept inside. She'd never allowed herself to consider the parts of sex that came between chaste kisses and the act itself, an act her wolf found appealing. Left to her own devices, the animal would have her on her stomach already, hips raised in offering for a joining that had always struck Joan as unappealingly savage.

Seamus's kiss wasn't savage, but it was demanding. His tongue slicked against hers, twisting pleasure and need into a tense ball that tugged at her with every stroke.

Too soon, he broke away, panting. "Sorry. That was..."

"A real kiss?" Oh, how breathless she sounded. Dazed, too, which would have stung her pride more if she could have dragged her gaze from his mouth.

He smiled suddenly. "A real kiss, that's for goddamn certain."

She wasn't ready to face the depressing realities of the world again. Not yet. This time she knew what he wanted and gave it to him, her lips on his, her mouth open and eager. The taste of him enchanted her, as did the rough scratch of stubble against her skin.

His hand slid around to the back of her head and held her still while his tongue tangled with hers. Then his mouth skimmed her cheek. "Joan."

If she kept her eyes closed, she could pretend the world began and ended with their tiny little cove. "Yes?"

His next words broke the spell. "Someone's coming."

Seamus heard only one person, on foot, moving quickly

and quietly but not sneaking. He rose and put Joan behind him as Victor ducked around the wide trunk of a precariously leaning tree. "We got trouble. A mile out and making a lot of noise. Don't think they're expecting much of a fight here."

"Damn it. Get everyone who can't fight into the big cave, the one with the narrow passage through the back."

"Already on it." Victor's gaze flicked to Joan and back almost too fast to mark. "I sent all of her people there. A few of the men are mostly healed up, but I figured they'd make a better last line of defense."

Joan stepped around him, her back stiff and her shoulders set in a stubborn line Seamus was already beginning to recognize. "How many?"

Victor glanced at him, clearly unsure if he should answer. Seamus stared him down. "They're her people. Answer the lady."

That earned him a tiny frown, and a slightly disapproving one for Joan. "Guy thinks there's only a few of 'em, based on the noise, but he's gone back out to try and get a closer look in case there're more coming in."

"Did he describe them?"

"Wolves, Miss Fuller. They were wolves."

If Joan heard the undercurrent of exasperation in his voice, she gave no sign as she pivoted to look up at Seamus. "Do you have enough men to deal with the threat?"

He nodded, already gathering the blanket into his arms. "Unless they're armed with something more mystical than guns or teeth."

She hesitated, her indecision obvious in the tight set of her jaw and the uncertainty in her eyes.

He gestured to Victor. "Put them all in the small chamber. We'll block it, and if the fight gets to be too much, they can

48

come out and help us."

Victor nodded and spun sharply. "I'll get it moving."

Seamus tucked the blanket over his arm and grasped Joan's shoulders. "It's just to be safe. If we can't handle it..."

"I can fight as a wolf," Joan whispered, clutching at his arms. "I've won challenges. I had to, to survive. If you need me, if you need help at all..." Her fingers tightened, and he knew how much the next words meant to her. "Protect my people."

He kissed her one last time, a quick promise more than anything else. "Can you run like this?"

A wild heat rose in her eyes before she pulled it back with obvious effort. "As fast as I need to."

"Then come on."

The run back was quick, but it took long enough for Seamus to go over the possibilities in his head. Most of them weren't good—they could be outnumbered, easily overwhelmed—but he forced himself to stay as calm as possible. Joan would be able to sense roiling power, and it would needlessly scare her.

She was already scared enough.

To her credit she didn't show it. Not a hint of her fear upset the serene, confident expression she fixed in place when they reached the caves. He could almost see her power twisting in as she gathered reserves from God knew where and squared her shoulders. "If you need help..."

"Go, Joan." A very personal sense of urgency compelled him to guide her toward the narrow opening in the back of the cavern. "Try to keep everyone calm and quiet."

"I will."

As soon as Joan was out of easy earshot Victor appeared at his side, eyes narrowed. "She's trouble. You've got that look."

Seamus avoided his gaze as he stripped out of his vest and shirt. "What look?"

"The one you always get when you see some sweet little society dish." Victor's vest hit the ground. "Believe me, Whelan, she's not worth the trouble. I know her type."

"That so? Enlighten me, Victor."

"Alpha bitches are all the same underneath. Don't know how to give an inch even if their damn fool lives depend on it."

As if Victor would do anything differently. "So she's got plenty in common with both of us, then."

Dark brown eyes glinted angrily in the thin light from the moon. "It's our job to protect them. Women like her spit on everything that's good about who and what we are."

Women like her were doing the best they could. Seamus wrapped one hand in the front of Victor's shirt. "I know you mean well and you're a good man, but if you don't shut your face, I'm going to pummel you."

Victor outweighed him by twenty pounds of muscle, but the angry power roiling inside the other man couldn't eclipse his own. Victor's mouth tightened as he held up both hands in clear defeat. "She's all yours."

"No, these people are all *hers*, and she wants to keep them safe. Surely you can respect that." Seamus turned to where Norman stood, watching the beach and woods beyond from the mouth of the cave. "Anything yet?"

"No sign of Guy," the man drawled, "but he's keepin' watch."

"There might have been time to—" A piercing howl rent the night. *Warning.* "Get ready."

Victor cursed and shucked his pants. Norman undressed just as fast, and magic swelled as both called on their wolves, the change flowing over them in a ripple of fur.

His wolf senses were far keener than his human ones, and Seamus could hear the snarls and snaps of the approaching attackers. There could be no more than a handful, few enough not to pose a problem.

Guy burst out of the trees first, a large white wolf with gray markings who darted past the cave just slowly enough to be seen before cutting back around to come up from the intruders' left flank. Norman shot in the opposite direction, paws silent on the rock-strewn ground as he disappeared into the trees.

The strong black wolf who was Victor stayed at Seamus's shoulder, tense and ready. This close, the trampling through the woods sounded like even fewer paws, and he wondered if they planned to attack in waves, one after the other.

Then the wolves broke out of the trees. There were only three of them, a large wolf flanked by two smaller ones. Seamus dug into the rocky sand and headed for the middle wolf.

It wasn't much of a fight. The largest wolf stumbled when they got close enough to feel the angry roil of Victor's power, and one of the smaller ones skidded to a stop and turned tail, bolting back into the woods. Seamus didn't spare him another thought; Norman and Guy would head him off.

The remaining interlopers didn't run. The larger lunged at Seamus, jaws snapping, but desperation and fear hung heavy enough in the air to choke them both.

Seamus fought only long enough to drive the wolf to the ground, then backed away, trusting that Victor would guard him. When he was far enough away, he dropped to his haunches and resumed his human form. "Who sent you?" he rasped.

The large wolf snarled at him. The smaller one whimpered from his spot on the ground in front of Victor. He was the one who changed, magic responding sluggishly and so slowly that his transformation looked agonizing. When it was done a young blond man knelt on the ground, eyes wide and terrified. "We were just supposed to get the girl."

Joan. "It's only the three of you?"

The boy shivered as a cold wind cut through the trees. "It was just supposed to be a bunch of women. They told us—"

Another snarl, and the large wolf lurched to his feet, gathered to pounce on his companion. Victor barreled into the wolf's side, knocking him back to the ground, and bared his teeth.

Seamus had to push down his own rage in order to ask, "They told you *what?*"

A choked noise ripped free of the blond boy, and he lowered himself closer to the ground. "I didn't have a choice. Lancaster told us not to touch the leader, b-but he said we could..."

He looked sick, which matched how Seamus felt. They had orders not to touch Joan, but watching them assault those in her care would hurt her in ways that far exceeded any physical threat. "What about Samuel, the alpha in Boston?"

The boy didn't answer. Joan did, her voice soft but carrying easily through the still night air. "He's in debt to Lancaster. As long as Edwin holds the purse strings, he makes the decisions."

Her presence in the face of danger sent a shaft of protective rage splintering through Seamus. "You were to stay in the cave," he growled.

"William is no danger to me."

Seamus could mark her approach by the soothing rush of magic as she stopped just behind him, leaving him between her and potential attack in spite of her calm words. "The one on the ground, however, is. He's one of Edwin's lackeys. A man with a taste for terrified girls."

Victor snarled. Soon, there would be no holding him back, not with that knowledge burning in his gut. "Take the boy and clean him up, Vic."

The young man—William—flinched, fear in his scent and in his eyes. "I don't know anything else. I swear."

Joan stepped forward again, her arm brushing Seamus's. "He's not going to torture you, William. No one here blames wolves for doing what they must to survive their alphas."

Victor *wouldn't* hurt him, though probably not for lack of motivation. "Vic?"

Magic ripped through the clearing as Victor shifted forms, his change flowing over him with a speed only one born a werewolf enjoyed. He stayed crouched on the ground, his gaze fixed on the remaining wolf. "This one doesn't deserve mercy."

He didn't, but he also didn't deserve the death Victor would give him, either. "The boy?" Seamus prompted.

Victor rose. "On your feet, puppy."

William looked like he might piss himself, but he obeyed. Then he looked at Joan. "I—I remembered one other thing."

She started forward, but Seamus held her back with one arm. "What is it?"

His gaze shot from Joan, who was bristling, to Seamus, and apparently judged Joan to be the less intimidating party. "There's a compass. It's with our clothes, a few miles back. Lancaster had it enchanted so it always leads to you."

More magic, and it lifted the hair on the back of Seamus's neck. He looked at Victor. "Maybe the wizard Guy knows can do something with that, if we can get in touch with him."

Victor curled a hand around the boy's arm. "Take me to where you left the compass."

The remaining wolf snarled and lunged for Joan, teeth bared and ready to snap. Years of fighting, of honing reflexes already sharpened by the wolf inside, spurred Seamus's reaction. He grabbed the wolf's head, unmindful of those snapping teeth, and twisted quickly, cracking his neck.

William staggered, and might have hit the ground if Victor hadn't dragged him bodily toward the woods. Joan simply stared at the prone wolf body, face impassive in the silvery moonlight. "Are you injured?" she asked Seamus finally.

Her heart pounded, but it wasn't fear that bridged the space between them. He fought to keep his own body from reacting. "I'm fine."

"I'm relieved to hear it." The words held a slight tremor, and he could feel the hunger of her wolf and her own rejection of it. "I should check on the others."

He wanted to stop her. He wanted to chase her again, like he had earlier.

So he stepped back, far enough that he could no longer sense her racing heart or the need that mirrored his own. "We can talk about this threat later."

"Of course." Her gaze roamed his face, then slipped lower, quick and furtive, as if she couldn't quite stop herself. The darkness couldn't hide the blush that rose in her cheeks as she turned abruptly. "Whatever you think is best. I'll—I'll be in the cave."

He had to turn to keep from following her. His frustration wanted to evidence itself in short, barked orders, but he was alone in the clearing.

Chapter Four

Her skin felt too tight, and inside-out too. Her nerves might as well be on the outside, laid bare to every brush of fabric, every teasing caress of wind. Too much sensation and not nearly enough. Never enough, because it was fabric and air, not rough hands and a hot mouth.

She was in danger. Serious, mortal danger, pursued by a madman who had leveled magic at her, and the twisting in her guts was the unbearable ache of need, not the sharp stab of fear.

On days like this, with her body beyond her control and held hostage to instincts she barely understood, Joan hated being a werewolf.

The cave was abuzz with nervous chatter and movement, the girls repacking their belongings and the men shifting bedrolls and blankets. They'd have to move, of course, though where Seamus intended to lead them next was only of passing interest.

Joan would not be with them.

If that terrifying moment in the clearing had given her anything, it was the peace of absolute trust. Her instincts might have reacted with embarrassing and appalling arousal to the show of brutal strength, but it didn't detract from the truth of the matter—Seamus would protect her people. He would keep them safe. She believed it with everything inside her, wolf and human alike.

It made leaving easier. Not easy—she couldn't walk lightly into the hands of the enemy, knowing what likely awaited her in Boston. She'd be a suitable distraction, though, and she was the only one they truly wanted. Once enough time had passed to know her people were free, she'd escape her prison or die trying.

There was an unexpected serenity in that knowledge. Enough to make it easy to move amongst the girls and give comfort where comfort was needed. Few needed it. Edwin's castoffs all had one thing in common—an appreciation for rakish men. There were certainly plenty of those to be found among Seamus's associates.

She found Simone shoving clothes into a bag, surprisingly unappreciative of those rakish men. "The tall one is an ass," she muttered. "I asked him what happened, and he tripped all over himself to reassure me that you were fine, that we're all fine. He didn't bother to actually answer my question. Like I need to be protected from the truth."

The tall one had to be Victor, who'd shown no particular warmth to Joan herself. "I don't think he has much faith in the sense of women."

"I have faith in the size of the hole he'll have in his head if he tries to 'there there, little lady' me again."

Simone was furious, angrier than Joan had ever seen her before, and it offered another whisper of peace. Simone wouldn't roll over for Seamus's men just because they were stronger. She'd fight if she had to. The girls would still have a protector.

Of course, that didn't help Simone in the short term. "Ignore him. The other men seem more amiable. Seamus is almost reasonable, for an alpha."

That melted some of Simone's ire. "He likes you."

Denial would be foolish at this juncture. "I know. Power calls to power. It always does."

She rolled her eyes. "Yes, that's almost certainly it. Except that it isn't at all, and you know it."

After everything that had happened, Joan should have grown past blushing. Yet warmth filled her cheeks as she knelt to help Simone store the last of her belongings. "This is neither the time nor place for romance. Keeping us safe is my only concern."

"The heart will not be contained." Simone delivered the flowery words in a matter-of-fact tone as she fastened the heavy bag and lifted it.

"Mine will be." Joan looked up at her closest friend and tried to find words that wouldn't rouse suspicion. "You need to know, Simone. I'm in more danger than most. They can't let me get away with the things I've done. I need you to promise me that if anything happens—"

Simone cut her off. "You're not thinking of doing anything foolish, are you, Joanie?"

Answering directly would reveal the lie, but Joan had grown up in the polite society of evasive small talk. "You said yourself that Seamus is interested. Do you honestly think an alpha like him would let me?"

"I think he doesn't know you like I do."

Only one distraction left. "I kissed him."

Simone froze. "You did not."

"On the beach." The heat of his fingers still felt branded on the back of her neck, as if that spot held the secrets of everything she needed from him. "It—it was very pleasant. Unexpectedly so, in fact."

Her friend hesitated. "I'm...not entirely sure what that means. That you want to do it again?"

Admitting the truth didn't matter now. "Desperately. I know it's not the place or the time, but when he kissed me, I didn't care. I always thought I was more sensible than that."

Simone simply blinked at Joan. "Well."

It wasn't quite the reaction Joan had expected. "Well?"

She shrugged. "You like him too. What are you going to do about it?"

"Nothing. I'm going to finish packing our things, and we're going to get in the cars and drive. One of the men has an acquaintance who might be able to hide us for a time using magic. I'll worry about kissing and feelings when we're safe."

"That's a plan, I guess." But Simone had already been distracted by Victor's entrance. "Hey! I want to talk to you."

Joan started to turn, but caught enough bare skin out of the corner of her eye to whip back around. "Simone, anything you have to say can wait until he's dressed."

A thoroughly amused, thoroughly male chuckle echoed in the confining space. The impossible man was laughing at her, as if modesty and courtesy were childish trivialities. Annoyance stiffened her spine, and she pivoted again and let him feel the full thrust of her power along with her temper. "You may dislike me as you please, but you *will* show the ladies respect. And that includes wearing clothing."

"It doesn't bother me in the least." Simone shrugged and crossed her arms over her chest.

Victor's gaze traveled from Joan to Simone, where it lingered with something approaching amused affection. His dark hair fell over his forehead as he nodded and took a step back, a clear sign of retreat. Then he turned on his heel and strode away, and even Joan had to admit that naked expanse of his well-muscled back was distracting, if you favored large men carved from stone.

Simone watched him, and she seemed to have forgotten altogether that she meant to talk to him. "Did Seamus mention where we're going?"

"I haven't had a chance to ask." Nor would Joan find out, because not knowing would be important later. What she didn't know she wouldn't be able to reveal, after all, and she wasn't foolish enough to believe the Boston alpha couldn't break her if he set his mind to it.

A chill claimed her at that thought, and a clawing claustrophobia with it. "Do you have the bags? I should check that everything's arranged."

"Sure. I'll look in on Elise too."

Elise would have a child soon, and Joan might never get to see her. She'd never find out if the tentative flirtation between the two youngest wolves might blossom into love, or if Simone's frustration with Victor might cover an interest the woman fought to hide.

Worst of all, there would be no goodbyes. But she could say the one thing that mattered, so she threw her arms around Simone and held her friend tight. "I wouldn't have managed this without you. Not any of it."

"We're not there yet," she answered grimly. "These men are so sure of themselves, but...I don't know. We have a long way to go."

They both did.

He'd known she was going to leave and that he'd have to follow.

Seamus stripped off the last of his clothes and called the change. It came easily, testament to the harsh emotions roiling inside him. He snarled and left the stopped caravan behind.

Victor would take care of everything. Seamus had spoken with him briefly, keeping his questions and instructions just vague enough to limit the man's suspicion. They hadn't been back on the road for long, and when the rest of them discovered he and Joan had gone, there would be no doubt what had happened.

He wanted to be furious that she would risk herself this way, but understanding tempered his anger. What wouldn't he do to protect his men or those that belonged to him?

To protect *her*?

She was heading in the right direction, so he followed at a distance until she stopped in a glade by a small creek to rest and drink. He shifted back and spoke as he approached, his voice hoarse from strain. "Give me one reason why I shouldn't spank your ass."

The small, exhausted-looking wolf lifted her head and snarled at him.

"Don't look at me like that." He sank down beside her. "Gray hair. You're going to give me gray hair, and I'm far too young for it."

She circled around him slowly, her paws rustling against the leaves. She stopped somewhere behind him, and power rose tired and sluggish. Her voice sounded every bit as rough as his own when she spoke, edged with sorrow and pain and magic. "You know I'll run again. Edwin can't let me make a fool of him like this. If we find one wizard, he'll find three. It will never end."

"So we find a way to fix it that doesn't involve you taking a powder, especially by yourself."

He felt the first brush of her skin against his bare back as she huddled closer, shivering in the cold night air. "Please, Seamus. Let me go. It may not be pretty, but they probably won't kill me, and they'll bore of me eventually. I can survive anything they do if I know you're keeping my people safe."

"Not just here to save you, Joan." He leaned back, just enough to press his skin more fully to hers. "I'm saving myself too. You might survive what happens to you, but I wouldn't."

A small hand slid over his shoulder, and her forehead pressed against his neck. "You hardly know me. You can't care so much."

But he did, and so did she. Seamus covered her hand with his and laughed a little. "Are you going to argue with me now?"

"Are you going to force me to?"

"Depends, some. You still want to run off by yourself?"

"I never wanted to." Her lips grazed the spot between his shoulder blades as she talked, each word a teasing kiss. "I know what the alphas in Boston are forgetting. Being dominant isn't about getting what you want."

"No, it isn't." It was about a hundred little things like comfort and family, as well as the bigger things—like protection. All the things he couldn't think of with her lips on his skin. "Joan."

Her lips pressed against him more firmly, no accidental kiss this time. "Tell me there's another way, and I'll take it. But I'm not going back to my people. Not until I know Edwin's done looking."

She was probably trying to scramble his brain so he'd agree with her, but he didn't care. "I didn't say anything about going back, did I?"

"Thank you." Her fingers tightened around his hand, clinging to him. "I—I don't have a plan that doesn't involve getting caught. I was going to wait at the cave until they used their magic to find me. I think Edwin will come with them this time. He'd want to see me taken care of personally."

It was as good as anything else. "We left some supplies

there. Come on. We'll dress and talk."

The warmth of her body against his vanished, but he didn't feel the corresponding swell of magic. After a few tense, silent moments she sighed. "I think I'm too tired to change again so quickly."

He picked her up and carried her.

There were no women's clothes at the cave, but Seamus managed to find a set of boys' trousers and a small shirt. "Put these on while I start a fire."

She accepted them in silence and slipped away toward the back of the cave. The fire pit was still warm, and it took him only minutes and a few fresh logs to stir it back to life. Outside, dawn was just beginning to break, but it would take hours for the sun's warmth to penetrate the shadows of the cave.

Joan returned, wearing the odd-fitting clothing and dragging two heavy blankets. "They were folded in the back. I shook them out to make sure nothing had taken up residence."

"Good idea. We'll lay them out by the fire."

Soon enough she'd created a little nest, with one blanket folded to provide padding from the cold stone floor. She wrapped one side of the other around her shoulders, then peered up at him with a look that dared him to comment on what she said next. "I saw some bottles too. I believe I finally understand the allure of applying liquor to a case of nerves."

A dangerous thing for a teetotaler like her to be thinking. "You want to tie one on, I'm not going to stop you. But maybe we could talk first."

Something like disappointment flickered across her face, then vanished. "Yes, I suppose that's the responsible thing to do."

Sympathy and guilt tugged at him. "I was also hoping to kiss you again, but I make it a point never to kiss drunk women."

Her eyes widened, and he seemed to have startled her into a smile. "How disappointingly upstanding. And here I thought you were a total scoundrel."

"Not quite, sweetheart."

"It would be better if you were. I could resist a scoundrel."

"No need to resist me." He offered her his easiest smile. "Just say the word."

For a heartbeat he thought she would, the longing in her eyes was that sharp. Instead color filled her cheeks and she looked away, suddenly shy. "We need to talk."

"What would you like to talk about?"

"Our plan. We'll have an advantage in that Edwin is unlikely to be willing to kill me outright. He needs to punish me in front of the others. To regain control."

She was saying that Lancaster meant to break her. Seamus clenched his hands into fists as rage splintered through him, and he forced himself to take a deep breath and focus. "That leaves me, and he'll likely want to dispose of me as soon as possible. Unless..."

"Unless?"

"Unless he figures it would hurt both of us more if he had me watch him...punish you."

The words made her clutch more tightly at the blanket. "I think that's a distinct possibility. Though if he concludes that I've developed any affection for you, it's just as likely that he'll try to take you apart piece by piece and force me to watch."

"Either way, it buys us some time."

"Time to fight?"

She relished the idea, and it sparked something primitive inside him. "That's right. Time to fight."

Joan turned her attention to the fire, her expression turning thoughtful. "I can fight...but that's dangerous. What if the worst happens? Will your people help mine find a safe place to settle?"

He'd left strict instructions that Victor wasn't to wait for his return before taking Joan's people to safety. "Guy's grandfather owns an island. We've been buying it up, bit by bit. Hell, we might own it all by this point. There's nothing there, but it's small enough to ward and build a colony of sorts."

Her eyes drifted shut. "Thank you, Seamus. I can't—after all this time, I can't tell you how much it means to know... To know—"

Tears rolled down her cheeks. "Hey." Seamus rose and circled the fire to sink down beside her. "Hey, it's all right. They're going to be okay."

"I know." Her voice trembled, but the tone was one of relief, not distress. She leaned into him, curled close and wrapped an arm around his neck. "Adam tried, but he could never understand. He protected them because he wanted to, because he's a good man under all his vices. He never understood that I didn't have the same choice."

"I know."

"You understand."

"That protecting them isn't a choice? That it tears you up inside when you feel like you can't get it done?" Her skin was soft under his fingers. "I understand, sweetheart."

"Yes, you do." She stroked the back of his neck before sliding her hand up to drift through his hair. "Tell me something about yourself. All I know is that you're a werewolf, and friends with Gavin, and that your associates are all such handsome scoundrels that I imagine I'll find every last one of my girls in love when I get back to them."

"Hopefully, the boys know better." They didn't, but telling her they were likely to flirt with her charges would make her feel worse.

"Mmm. But you didn't answer my question."

He couldn't sneak anything past her, which meant he'd have to answer. "What do you want to know?"

She didn't answer at first. Her fingers continued their meandering path up and down his neck as she curled closer, dragging the thick blanket with her. Finally she blew out a breath and tilted her head back. "Do you want to kiss me as desperately as I want to kiss you?"

His body tightened, but he managed to check his groan. "I kept you away from the rum, didn't I?"

"I suppose you did." She brushed her lips along the line of his jaw. "How did you become a werewolf?"

If he told her the whole terrible story, it would cool her ardor quickly. "Women aren't the only ones purposefully changed to suit an alpha. There was one back home who needed more men. More fighters."

"Back home. Ireland?"

"Dublin."

"How long ago?"

He'd almost fooled himself into believing he'd lost count of the years, but the date came easily. "1891. November twelfth."

She wasn't slow at math. "Forty-two years ago. I suppose I'm still not used to how deceptive aging can be among those not quite human. I thought you were my age."

"No." He smiled to distract her. "Quite a bit older, actually."

"A lecherous old man, then." Her hand drifted up to cup his

cheek. "We have nothing to do but wait. A kiss can't be that irresponsible, can it? Just a kiss?"

The ultimate irresponsibility, and he hoped he would be the only one to pay the price. "Not at all. Kiss me, sweet Joan."

She did, brushing her mouth against his in the lightest of caresses and retreating before he could react. Her fingers slid around to the back of his neck before she parted her lips and kissed him again.

This time, with no one but them in the cave, her almost clumsy eagerness barely registered, but heat flared in him with undeniable intensity. *Careful, boy. Don't frighten her.*

And the full force of his desire would scare her, no matter how instinctively attracted to him she happened to be.

That she *was* instinctively attracted was certain. A tense, nervous energy trembled inside her, a quiet battle between woman and wolf. It evinced itself in a dozen tiny clues—her fingernails scraping against his skin before she relaxed her hand, her teeth almost closing on his lower lip with every noise she made.

Seamus took a deep breath and slid his hand into her hair. Gentle force urged her head back, and he pressed careful kisses to her cheeks and jaw. "Relax."

"I can't. I want—" She shuddered as his mouth found the spot where her jaw met her throat, fingers clenching almost painfully around his arm. "*She* wants. She wants more than I'm ready for."

"Sex?"

"Sex. Mating. Everything." Her lips brushed his ear. "She's infatuated."

Her words made it hard for him to speak his own. "Neither of us is ready for that right now, Joan. But the kissing is good."

Joan pulled back, a furrow between her eyebrows and a

tiny, puzzled smile curling her kiss-swollen lips. "I don't know what to make of you, Seamus Whelan."

"Of course you don't. A true cad of my caliber would have your pants off by now, right?"

"I'm more concerned with what you'll do when I take leave of my senses and try to remove yours."

Fantasies were made of stuff like that. "No, you won't."

It was a command, and it worked magic on the wolf inside her. She went liquid in his arms, smiling up at him with a sweet, open trust. "Not if you'll kiss me instead."

The trust made him ache as much as the soft press of her mouth and body. Her lips parted under his, and he teased her with his tongue, just enough to show her how good it could be.

She was breathless when she finally pulled away and dropped her head to his shoulder. "Do you think we're safe here until tonight?"

"Depends." They could come looking for her soon, or it could be days. "Want to get some rest?"

"I think I ought to. But if the others don't arrive—"

"You're getting a little ahead of yourself, aren't you?"

Joan was implacable. "If we're going to fight, maybe we should go back home. To the farmhouse, I mean. They'll find us eventually, but Astrid set warning wards around the property. Even if—even if she's not alive anymore, I should be able to activate them with a little blood. We'll know they're coming before they reach us."

It would be useful, since he had no idea who—or what—they'd send after them. "After we get some sleep and make sure Gavin and Adam aren't showing up here."

She nodded against his shoulder, then pulled back and stared up at him with a wobbly smile. "Thank you for coming after me. For caring enough to want to help."

He indulged himself by stroking the back of his hand over the curve of her cheek. "Anytime you need me, sweetheart."

Her eyelids drooped, and her breath came out on a shaky sigh. "Be careful what you offer. I might just take you up on it."

With a woman like her, a strong alpha, the threat was nothing short of a miracle. "I'll hold you to it."

Joan smiled and curled closer to him, but the soft shiver that shook her body didn't seem to spring from arousal. She confirmed it a moment later with a whisper. "It's cold."

It would be easier to warm the smaller, enclosed area at the back of the cavern. Safer too, and perhaps they could both sleep instead of taking turns at watch. The only problem was that the smoke from their fire would give away their position.

Unless they didn't need the fire. "Do you ever sleep as a wolf?"

"On rare occasions. It might be wise now. If someone does come upon us, I'm not a very effective fighter as a human."

"I meant more for warmth. We could move into the smaller space. It would hold heat more efficiently, but we'd be safer without the smoke from the fire."

"Oh." She nodded and eased back. "It's a good idea."

She rose slowly, as if the movement took more effort than she wanted to show. Seamus carefully covered the fire as she eased through the crevice in the cavern wall.

It took only moments to bank the flames, but he waited until magic swelled through the cave before standing to shed his clothes. The change came over him, and he padded back to join her in the smaller space of the secondary cavern.

He considered blocking the opening, but it would be difficult to do from the inside. It would take intruders long enough to spot the crevice, and they'd have time to react. That was really all they needed.

Well, not all. Seamus settled to the ground and curled around Joan, who lifted her head to bump her nose against his muzzle.

It was a purely instinctive gesture, one of deference and submission, and it sent a protective shudder racing through him. He'd promised Dubois he would keep them safe, all of them, but Joan was different. She was *his*, and she seemed to know it.

As if oblivious to the storm she'd set off inside him, she wiggled closer until she was curled tight against his side, her head tucked under his chin. Sleep claimed her quickly, her sides rising and falling slowly, her breath ruffling his fur.

He could keep her safe. That was all that mattered now.

Chapter Five

The farmhouse was eerily empty, devoid of the chattering of female voices and men calling back and forth. Joan stood in the middle of what had been their dining room and examined the evidence of their hasty departure the day before.

As far as she could tell in the darkness, all was as they'd left it. First aid supplies and ruined towels lay scattered across the long table that Adam had built himself, a solid expanse that had seated twenty. Not everyone had been able to sit there, not in the later years when more and more had fled the Boston pack and taken refuge at the farm, but in the early years they'd shared family dinners, rife with laughter and warmth.

The table had been shoved against the wall, the benches that went with it upended and pushed aside. Joan righted one of them, straining against the heavy weight even with the strength that had come to her with her new life. When it sat upright she let herself sink down, resting her body as her numb gaze swept the room again.

Exactly as they'd left it, and until that moment she hadn't realized how desperately she'd clung to the hope that they'd find some evidence of Adam or Gavin or the rest of her people. Proof that they'd been here, that they'd escaped and were scrambling to make a late rendezvous at the cave.

Nothing undisturbed. Joan wrapped her arms around herself and shivered, more relieved than she wanted to admit when Seamus returned from his exploration of the house. She knew the answer, but she still asked. "No signs that anyone's been here?"

He hesitated, regret and worry thinning his lips. "No, I'm sorry."

Edwin might have them all, then. She hardened her heart against fear and rose. "If no one else is here, we should set the wards."

"How do we do that?"

"Upstairs." She started toward the back of the house, trusting him to follow. The stairs creaked as she eased up them, leading him past two dormitory-style rooms and through the narrow doorway that separated the original house from the newest addition.

Only three rooms, but all were spacious and well appointed, mostly with furniture Adam had carved himself. A smaller bedroom for Adam and two larger ones on either side of the modern bathroom, where Joan could run herself a bath for the first time in longer than she cared to consider. She let her fingers brush over her own door, imagining the wide bed she'd shared with Simone and how comfortable it would be to curl up with Seamus and ignore the world for the rest of the night...

No. Common sense pushed her to the end of the hallway and into the neatly organized bedroom Maggie and Astrid had shared. In the corner sat a small table, and on it a clear glass ball surrounded by stubby dark candles. A fortuneteller's crystal ball, a frivolity Adam had purchased as a joke and that Astrid had turned to practical use. That was Astrid to the core—imminently, ruthlessly practical.

Joan stopped beside the table and picked up the knife sitting next to the candles. No ornate dagger or mystical blade, just one of the knives from the kitchen sharpened to a keen edge. "Blood keys it. But without Astrid here, I don't think we can turn it off again without breaking the crystal."

"Can't see any reason we'd have to." Seamus laid his hand over hers, over the one holding the knife. "Do you want me to do it?"

"Both of us," she whispered. "In case we're not together when they arrive. Whoever bloods it will feel the warning. It's like a magical shock."

He nodded, tightened his fingers around her hand and drew the blade quickly across his palm. Blood welled from the wound in a thin, crimson line.

She didn't hesitate before doing the same. The knife was so sharp that the cut stung more than hurt, or maybe the discomforts of the past weeks had inured her to pain.

Together they pressed their hands against the clear crystal. Joan gasped when hot magic raced through her, tightening her skin until she was painfully aware of the warm press of his fingers over hers and the solid bulk of his body.

He hissed in a breath, his eyes wild. "Is it supposed to feel like this?"

Activating the wards had always brought a little zip of heat, but never anything like this. "I don't know. Maybe it's too much magic." She opened her fingers and the knife clattered to the table as she turned and pressed her body to his. "Or maybe it's just us."

He grabbed her, his hands twisting in her too-large clothes as he drew her to him. His mouth descended over hers, open and questing, and the heat exploded in a rush of longing and need strong enough to overcome any polite rules of human society.

She tore her mouth from his and panted for breath as she stepped back, dragging him with her. "My bedroom. We passed it."

He stumbled after her, his hand shaking. "Yes."

Before she'd been nervous, too aware of her carefully guarded virtue and how foolish she would seem, fumbling like a young girl who'd never touched a man. Now he seemed just as clumsy, strong hands a short step from wild as they clenched in her borrowed shirt. The fabric ripped as they made it into the hallway and crashed against the opposite wall, and Joan gasped and twined her arms around his neck. "Take me to bed. *Please*, Seamus."

He lifted her against him, urging her legs around his hips. Two quick steps took him to the bedroom door, and he kissed her again as he shoved through it and headed for the bed.

He dropped her onto it and ripped open his shirt. "Tell me you're ready for this."

This time she could look her fill, trace the hard muscles of his chest with her gaze until her fingers ached with the need to touch. She came up on her knees and reached for him, flattening her palms against his bare skin, and nearly moaned at the fire that might burn her if she stayed too close. "If you'll show me what to do. I've never—"

"I know." He caught her hands and tugged them up so he could kiss her palms. "Slow and easy. I promise."

She frowned and curled her fingers, scratching the sides of his cheeks as she leaned up to bite his chin. "Not too slow. It will hurt a little the first time. I don't care. We'll do it again."

He took a deep, shuddering breath. "Never another first time, Joan. Trust me."

Trust was easy. Telling herself to slow down, less so. It felt as if everything they'd been through had led to this moment, to the total breakdown of what remained of her strict upbringing and the rules she'd taken upon herself to abide by even in a world gone mad. It brought perfect clarity, being at peace with the wolf inside her, something she'd only felt before when she'd

73

Moira Rogers

fought for her life.

Now she was celebrating life. She slid her hands over his neck and the tight, coiled muscles of his shoulders to where his shirt still hung from his arms. Dragging it down brought his chest close enough for her to kiss it, pressing her lips to hot skin stretched taut over hard muscles. "If you don't show me what you want me to do, I'll make it up as I go along and it will be your own fault."

Seamus swore between clenched teeth and freed his arms from the tangled shirt. Then he cupped her head, guiding her mouth over his chest. "Doing a good job so far."

Joan shivered and eased her lips apart before touching the tip of her tongue to his chest. "That?"

He groaned and eased them both down to lie on the bed. "That."

His helpless need in the face of her attentions stirred her so much that she closed her teeth on his skin, marking him in a primal, desperate claiming. *You are mine, Seamus Whelan. Whether you know it or not, you're mine.*

Another groan, and he wrestled her arms up over her head and pinned them to the bed. "Slow down, sweet Joan. Let me make it good."

"It *is* good," she whispered, rubbing her legs together as a soft ache centered low in her body. "How much better do you plan to make it?"

His lips brushed her cheek and mouth. "So good you'll think you can't stand it."

She tried to tug one hand free and whimpered when she couldn't. "My shirt. I want to take off my shirt. I'm too warm."

"Don't move. I'll do it." Seamus trailed his fingers slowly down her arms and began freeing the buttons lining the front of the garment.

74

Obeying him thrilled her in a way she hadn't anticipated. She curled her fingers around the pillow under her head to quash the temptation to reach for him. "I want your hands on my skin so desperately."

He parted the rough fabric and slid his palm over her stomach. "Do you trust me?"

She felt no hesitation, no confusion. Woman and wolf both knew the answer. "Yes."

His hair fell over his eyes as he raised his head and smiled at her. "Then let me love you."

Love. Not what he'd meant, but the word shook through her regardless, a promise of what she could have if she could just surrender to it. "Yes. I'd like that."

Seamus touched her gently, though his hands trembled on her skin. He stripped off the shirt and her oversized shoes before loosening the belt that cinched her borrowed pants. The whole time, he watched her face, gauging her reactions with a hot gaze. "This is what a woman like you deserves, especially at a time like this."

"A woman like me?" She liked those words less. "What sort of woman am I, Seamus?"

"A beautiful woman." He unbuttoned her pants. "Sweet, sexy. Gorgeous."

"Oh." Warmth rose in her cheeks, and she closed her eyes. "I thought you were going to say prissy, difficult and virginal. Or at least be thinking it."

His eyes lit with laughter. "No, sweet Joan. Only someone who'd never glimpsed the fire under your very prim exterior would consider you prissy."

With her shirt gone and her pants undone, she was far from prissy or prim. "It was safer to be thought of as cold. I acted frozen, and I started to feel that way."

"You're not cold," he whispered. "So far from it, I ache just looking at you."

"You make me melt." She touched his cheek, ran her fingers through the rakish fall of his hair. "You make me feel alive."

"Yes?" He reached into the baggy pants she wore.

Her body trembled. She tugged at his hair, wanting to feel his mouth on her skin. "You make me feel wild."

He gave her his mouth, along with a soft, teasing lick just under her collarbone. She arched and pressed closer, needing his heat, his touch, needing it all more than her next breath.

He made a soothing noise, his breath blowing hot against her skin as he stroked her hip and slipped his hand down between her thighs.

Nervousness was impossible under his gentle touch. She'd been prepared for fast—had wanted it, even—but now she reveled in the delicious, twisting tension he built higher with skillful caresses. Arousal had readied her, left her wet and aching and craving the illicit things she'd pretended so hard not to overhear when the girls put their heads together and whispered. It was all too easy to anticipate, to imagine his fingers, strong and sure, sliding inside her. His mouth, wicked and taunting, trailing down her body until his tongue drove her to madness.

He did put his fingers inside her, one and then another, probing. Stretching. Seamus lifted his head, his brow furrowed. "Damn, you're tight."

Her breath caught, and she clenched her fingers in his hair. "That seems—seems—" She couldn't even think of a retort, not when the persistent ache had become a need so sharp it hurt. Angling her hips helped, rocking up against him as she chased an elusive pleasure that remained just out of her grasp. "*Seamus.*"

His head dipped to hers again, just as he twisted his hand and stroked her with his thumb.

"Oh!" Firm lips muffled her gasp, but he took advantage of her parted lips and kissed her again, his tongue stroking over hers in time with the irresistible movement of his fingers and the dizzying press of his thumb.

He whispered her name against her mouth and probed deeper, his hand rocking more firmly. Restless squirming found a focus as his fingers brushed the perfect spot, a magical touch that curled her toes and tightened her fingers until she knew she was yanking at his hair in her desperation. "There, right there, don't stop—oh *please* don't ever stop—"

Seamus ducked his head and closed his teeth on her neck with a harsh growl.

Light exploded through the room—or maybe just behind her eyelids, though she couldn't remember squeezing her eyes shut. Every frantic sensation in her body pulled in tight, centering for one endless moment on the quick, almost rough circling of his thumb. In the next heartbeat it broke free, and she cried out, caught in the trembling grip of pleasure that rushed to the tips of her fingers and toes, only to retreat and do it again, and again, until nothing existed but joy and him.

His desperate groan vibrated against her throat, and he murmured encouraging words. "See? Good, Joan, so good."

"Yes..." She gasped in a breath and shifted her grip to his shoulders, nails scraping against his skin as she tried to bring him atop her. "Now. Take me now. I need you *now*."

He surged over her, his arms shaking as he braced himself above her and settled his hips on hers. "Careful."

She felt nothing but his bare skin against hers, and it was a mark of how lost she was that she couldn't remember him removing their pants. Later she might wonder, but now she followed instinct—human instinct, this time—and hooked her legs over his hips. "I'm strong enough to take you. Don't ever think I'm not."

"I know." He moved closer, the hard head of his erection almost pressing into her. "You're strong, and you're fierce. You're mine."

Joan dug her heels into his lower back, not fighting the growl that rose from deep in her chest, and swept the rest of her manners away with it. "Do you want me to say it? Do you want me to beg you to—to fuck me?"

Seamus drew in a sharp breath and bit her, his teeth scoring her lip. "Don't talk dirty when a man's trying to take it slow, love."

"If you don't like the things I'm saying, I suppose you should find a way to make me stop."

"Maybe I should." He kissed her and pushed forward, entering her slowly.

Too slowly.

Discomfort was inevitable and unimportant. Nothing compared to the daily pain of shifting to a wolf, or even the recent sting of sacrificing blood for magic. Joan dug her teeth into his lower lip and rocked up, so hungry for the hot, intimate press of his body inside hers that she needed all of him.

Finally, he drove forward, burying his body completely into hers, and froze. "Jesus Christ."

"See?" The word trembled, in spite of her attempt to sound as if the world wasn't spinning out of her grasp. "You're mine."

His arms flexed and shook as he levered his body up a little and looked down at her with shadowed eyes. "Tell me you're all right."

Pain was already a distant dream. Having his lean body stretched over hers could have been a dream, the very best kind. She touched his shoulders, smoothed her fingers along his sweat-dampened skin and nearly moaned at the tension trembling in his muscles as he fought to hold back.

No more holding back. Not for her, and not for him. "I won't be all right until I'm yours."

"You *are* mine, Joan." He pulled away and thrust into her again, the movement bordering on desperate. "You—Joan—"

"Seamus." The pleasure of his movements built that perfect tension again, and she closed her eyes and tilted her head back, riding the slow spiral instead of reaching for it. He'd bring her relief, bring her *release*, and all she had to do was trust him. She didn't even have to struggle to find his rhythm; every deep, steady thrust brought her hips up, awkwardly at first, but that awkwardness didn't last long after instinct kicked in.

Wild instinct. Not fully wolf or fully human, but both and neither. It was primal, ancient, whispering that this was life; the hot sweaty press of bodies, the heady pleasure and the warmth that kindled inside her and had nothing to do with the way her body tightened around him. Life wasn't money and manners, polite society and prim behavior. It was the way he murmured her name, hoarse with need but tender, the way his body strained into her, hungry and feral but leashed by gentle protectiveness.

Sex. Dirty, guilty glorious sex, and that something more that had come to life when he'd whispered, *Let me love you.*

He took her mouth again, his tongue plunging between her lips in a sensual echo of the joining of their bodies. Then he shifted his hips, angled them so that his next thrust shredded any ability to think, until she was oblivious to anything but the sensation of their bodies. Hers, straining upward, wild and needy; his, hard and hot inside her, rubbing against some quiet spot that made her blood pulse in her ears as she panted the first syllable of his name over and over, too breathless and lost to do more until tension boiled over and she cried out.

It was better than the first time. A hundred times better, a *thousand* times better, and she clutched at his shoulders until she was sure she'd drawn blood, clinging to the only solid thing left in a world shaking with pleasure.

A second later, his smooth rhythm faltered. Seamus dropped his face to her neck and bit her, muffling his groan as he jerked against her. His hands slid down her body, holding her tight. "*Joan.*"

Her throat throbbed under his teeth. Her skin tingled. She wrapped her arms and legs around his body, holding him tight against her, and sucked in a trembling breath. "Let's do it again."

His chuckle was low, and it tugged at something deep inside her. "You won't be saying that in the morning. Give yourself some time."

Joan laughed too, and it felt joyful. Free. She held up her hand, the one she'd used to activate the wards. A hint of blood smeared her palm, but the thin cut had knit shut, showing only a tiny fading scar. "If I didn't know better, I'd think you've never taken a virgin werewolf to bed before. We heal quickly, you know."

"I was accounting for that." He rolled carefully to his side and drew her back into his arms. "If you were human, I'd have said you needed a few days."

"If you say so." Truth be told, with peaceful languor settling in, moving seemed like a terribly unappealing proposition, something to be reserved for the imminent arrival of invaders. Unless... "You could always distract me by offering to draw a bath. The tub is big enough for you to join me, if you wanted."

Seamus laughed. "And how is that supposed to give you respite from my masculine attentions?"

"Is that what we're calling it?" She rubbed her cheek against his shoulder, pleased with the idea that he'd carry her

80

scent as a warning to other females. No one else could take what she'd claimed. "I would think a dangerous criminal like yourself would have all sorts of interesting words."

"Interesting, yes. Appropriate? Not so much."

Joan closed her eyes. "I'm tired of appropriate. I've been appropriate all of my life. I'd like to try being something else for a while."

He grasped her hand and wove their fingers together. "Some of us get along just fine without being appropriate, I suppose."

"It was all I had." With his arms around her, it felt safe to whisper the things she'd never told anyone, not even Simone. "The men of the pack hated me for not submitting. Everything was cruelty and violence and savage and inhuman. And sometimes I thought—I thought if I just clung hard enough, that maybe I could make a place for wolves who were still human."

His voice and touch softened. "It's not about still being human, Joan. It's about not being selfish, not thinking that being stronger means you get everything you want, even if you have to take it."

"I know that now." She turned and pressed her cheek to his chest, taking comfort in the steady beat of his heart. "I still want to make a place. A place where wolves can be...what they are. What we are."

At first, Seamus didn't speak. Then he sighed. "The island. We bought it from Guy's grandfather so we could set up there, have a place to—to lie low after all the smuggling. Figure out what we wanted to do."

She felt the first tentative thread of uncertainty. "And you didn't make plans to support so many."

"No," he admitted. "But that doesn't mean it can't be done.

81

Moira Rogers

It'd be a hard first winter, but if we made it through..."

"Most of my people are used to hard winters." All of them, in fact, except for her. Human status had held sway in the pack—those with means could escape mistreatment, after all, if only by fleeing. "I sent money with them. Cash and bonds, and a little gold. Enough to help buy supplies."

"That's the thing. We've got plenty of money, but you can't just buy things like shelter, not out there. We'll all have to work."

"Then we'll work. We'll learn what we need to do. Even the weakest of us is as strong as any human man."

"The physical labor might be the least of it, sweetheart."

"I don't understand."

Seamus kissed the top of her head. "It'll be isolated, and my men aren't like the ones your people are used to. There's not a weak one in the bunch, and that might be difficult to deal with."

Joan considered that just long enough to understand what Seamus couldn't. Edwin, for all his many, many vices, hadn't numbered unwilling women among them. Young, perhaps. Ripe for debauching. But never unwilling.

Even her newly formed resolution to ignore society's strictures couldn't overcome panic at the idea of being trapped on an island with a dozen earthy young women hungry for wicked men and a gang of former bootleggers who would surely seem like saviors straight out of a fairy tale. Left unchecked, all the women would be pregnant by spring.

She very nearly whimpered. "I think they'll get used to it more quickly than you think."

He choked on something that sounded like a laugh. Maybe he wasn't as oblivious as she'd thought. "Yes, they'll grow used to it very quickly, I should say."

82

Beyond her own discomfort, there were practical concerns. "I'll have to make it clear to them that this winter will be a trial. And perhaps you can impress upon your men the importance of being...careful. Most of my girls have never been treated with any sort of gentleness or respect by a strong male wolf. It's very heady."

"I'll tell the men to keep their hands to themselves."

"Or, if they can't, at least..." Judging by the heat in her cheeks, she was blushing furiously enough to be glowing. "I'm fairly certain there are...alternatives. Ways people can enjoy themselves without worrying about pregnancy."

Now he was undoubtedly laughing. "Yes, sweet Joan. There are ways." His voice dropped. "I'll show you a few."

She turned her head and bit his chest with just enough force to leave a mark. "You'll have to. I can't take the risk either. I have too much work to do."

He groaned and held her mouth close to his skin. "Right. We'll have to be more careful, then."

Be more careful. She soothed the mark she'd left with her tongue and bit him again, thrilling at the noise he made. A day ago she'd left her people behind, convinced she was walking to her own death. Even when Seamus had joined her, she hadn't really believed. She'd even considered taking him that night, in the woods on the ground, rutting with him like an animal because nothing mattered anymore.

Now it mattered. There was a future past the next week, if only they could get there. She moaned and lifted her head, sliding up his body to brush her lips over his. "I'm being careful. Do you understand?"

His body went rigid under hers. "Why do I get the feeling you're talking about more than making love?"

"Just...understand." She dropped her forehead to rest

against his. "You give me hope. I fought and fought and there was no end in sight, no reason to think I'd ever be doing anything but fighting. Just knowing there's something past fighting..."

Seamus pulled her up and sat, easing her legs to one side so he could settle her in his lap. "There's something past the fighting," he told her softly, his breath blowing against the damp hair at her temple. "There's me. Us."

It was almost a promise, a reckless one, considering what lay ahead. Joan didn't care. She curled more closely against him, resting her cheek on his shoulder as she marveled at the peace she felt, even in the face of everything yet to come. "Lots and lots of long, shared baths?"

"Keeping each other warm all winter long."

"You *are* quite warm. I suppose that makes you useful to have about."

He laughed. "Who needs a coal heater when you have a naked werewolf?"

"That's the conclusion I'm afraid everyone will come to soon enough."

His laughter subsided into a smile, but it held an edge. "My men will listen to what I say, or they'll answer to me. That includes making sure no one is hurt by the consequences because they couldn't keep their pants on."

The danger, the reckless confidence... Both were intoxicating, even as they stirred the need to test her strength against his own. "I know. We'll make it work."

"Yes." He tilted his head to hers. "Bath?"

"Bath." She needed to enjoy the luxurious tub while she could. Edwin would arrive soon enough, primed for a fight. He might have even enlisted the Boston alpha's assistance through the power of money and shared antipathy. Battle and bloodshed lay in her future...but not tonight.

Tonight she had Seamus. And hope.

Joan seemed surprised that he could cook, and Seamus took a moment to enjoy the relief that lit her face. There wasn't a damn thing about her that wasn't beautiful, and she was *his*.

The instinctive reaction she evoked should have scared the hell out of him, but the fact was that he liked her—a lot. It wouldn't take much for that attraction to blossom into more. All they needed was a little time.

Seamus set the skillet on the counter and pulled a knife from the drawer. "Want to learn how, or do you want to save the lessons for this winter?"

"This winter," she said without hesitation. "I'm a terrible cook. I think I might be able to learn to bake, with a patient teacher. Mary makes the most amazing pies."

"Then you'll have to talk to Mary about that. I can't bake for sh—" He broke off and cleared his throat. "At all. I can't bake at all."

Joan pursed her lips as if trying not to laugh. "Asking your men to keep their hands to themselves seems trying enough. I can overlook the occasional coarse language. You might recall I recently had a lapse of my own."

Even the memory heated his body. Joan, bucking under him, begging him to fuck her. "I recall very well."

"I thought as much." Pink tinged her cheeks as she looked back down at the list she'd been compiling. "I think I have everyone. If the alpha is holding Gavin and Adam and the others, it will be at Edwin's house. It's far enough out of the city to be discreet and has a fair bit of land attached. I think most of the pack's activities are based there now, though more out of necessity than choice. Edwin has the money, so he has the power."

A sad fact of human nature that had lately been exerting itself over werewolf nature more often than not. "And how does the alpha feel about that?"

"Bitter." She traced absent little whirling doodles along the edge of the paper without looking up. "I think...I think without me, they would have fought it out by now. But what the three of us stood for here—it was a threat to both of them, so they've been uneasy allies."

But they could work with that bitterness, perhaps even use it to remove Edwin from the alpha's reluctant graces. "I understand."

Her foot bounced under the table, proof of the restless energy that burned inside her. "It all comes back to the money. I think if Samuel could figure out a way to legally take Edwin's assets, he'd already be dead. But Edwin's not stupid. And he has a good lawyer."

Perhaps the alpha needed to consider working *outside* the law. "Their argument is theirs," he reminded her.

"Their argument is useful," she countered. "If I could just figure out *how*."

Seamus barely managed not to smile. She was sneakier than she gave herself credit for being, and he liked it. "I think you've got a bit of a rogue bottled up in you too, sweet Joan."

She finally looked up, and her eyes glinted with amusement. "Women have been using men's vices against them since men discovered vice."

"Mm-hmm." He cracked two more eggs into the bowl. "And what did they use against them before that?"

"Why would they need to? Men were angels. Now I'm thinking they might have been a bit boring too."

"Men have never been angels, sweetheart."

"I suppose not." Her pen scratched against the paper again, more idle doodles. "I'll enjoy learning about your vices, as long as I'm numbered among them."

His greatest vice, and he proved it by not being able to stop himself from crossing to the table to slide his fingers through her hair. "Tell me something."

She tilted her head back and smiled up at him. "Anything."

He nuzzled her cheek and relished the scent of her. "What are *your* vices?"

"I don't know." The pen clicked against the table and her hands smoothed along his cheeks. "I never allowed myself to have any, except pride. That's not a very fun one."

"Mmm, I'm partial to lust, myself."

Her lips found his ear, warm breath skating against him as she spoke. "You inspire lust in me."

"Better than wrath." He bent his head licked her earlobe gently.

Her breath caught on a tiny, startled noise and released on a sigh of pleasure. "You inspired a little of that too. Is it wrong to admit it makes the lust...sharper?"

"Wrong? No." Seamus closed his teeth on her ear. "A little naughty, yes."

That elicited a satisfyingly breathless gasp. Her fingers slipped down to curl in his shirt and her voice grew huskier. "I'll have you know, I am never naughty."

"No?" He couldn't resist the soft curve of her throat, so he dropped his lips to it. "Not ever?"

"Maybe once. Or twice. I might have to concede that our antics in the bathtub last night were a little outrageous."

Just thinking about having her under him again made his

blood heat. "Outrageous enough for you to need more time to recover?"

Joan laughed as her hand edged under his shirt, her nails dragging lightly over his skin. "If you don't stop treating me like I'm weak, we're going to have to detour into wrath. I can feel how strongly the magic burns in you. Can't you feel me?"

"Yes." Her magic soaked into every pore of his body, vibrating inside him as they spoke. "But what sort of lover would I be if I didn't concern myself over you?"

"Lover." Her voice turned the word into a caress. Her teeth closed on his ear, mirroring the way he'd nipped at her, and pleasure shuddered up his spine.

Seamus leaned over, trapping her against the wood. "Lover."

Joan eased her hand free and slid both up to hook under his suspenders. "I'm fine, Seamus. I'm aching for you."

He could tell. The scent of her body, earthy and aroused, tickled his nostrils and stirred his own body. "Tell me what you want."

She guided his suspenders down. "Everything."

There were plenty of things he could do to her, things she might never have heard of, but would love all the same. He grasped her hips, lifted her and turned to drop her on the counter. "Lean back."

"Bossy." She'd donned a loose men's shirt and a flowing skirt, claiming she wanted to be ready if they had to shift. Now she smiled wickedly as she lifted her fingers and tugged the top button of her shirt open, then the second, revealing the smooth curve of her breasts. "Do women just do whatever you tell them to?"

"Sometimes," he admitted.

The third button gave way, and the shirt slipped from her

shoulder. The fabric caught on her breasts, snug enough to show how tight her nipples were. "Do you like it when a woman does whatever you tell her to?"

He didn't bother to hide his feral grin as his hand grazed her inner thigh. "Sometimes."

Joan drew her legs together, trapping his hand, then leaned forward until her lips hovered over his. "That sounds like submission," she whispered, every word like a teasing kiss. She licked his lower lip and laughed. "I've listened to the gossip. I know that giving in to our instincts can make sex more...primal."

"You want primal?" Her shirt was like paper under his hands, and he tore the fabric free of her body, though he left it wrapped around her arms. "Say the word, sweet Joan."

She dragged in a breath and leaned into him, pressed her breasts to his chest with a shaky moan. "What word? Primal? Please?"

He chased her back until his body was stretched out over hers. "The word...is *yes.*"

"Yes." Her head fell back, and she didn't struggle, even though she could have easily torn her arms free of the tangle of her shirt. "Yes, yes, *yes—*"

She wore only plain cotton panties under the voluminous skirt, and Seamus tugged at them. "What other gossip have you heard?"

Wildness filled her eyes as she watched him. "That finding a man with a clever tongue is of paramount importance."

The cotton slid easily down her legs, and Seamus licked his lips. "You don't say."

"Are you going to show me why?"

He wanted to, not only to drive her wild, but to put his mouth to her body and taste her. "Yes."

She wet her lips, an adorable anticipation lighting up her face. "Right here on the counter?"

"You like the idea?"

"More than I should."

"Says who?" He teased her by grazing his fingertips over the sensitive flesh at the apex of her thighs as he bent closer. "That society you're always talking about?"

The sound of her shallow, strained breaths filled the kitchen as her legs inched apart in silent invitation. "I want it more than I thought possible."

"That's what I like to hear." This close, he could feel the heat of her on his tongue before he even touched her. And then he did.

Her breath caught and her knees knocked into his shoulders as she let out a choked noise that mixed pleasure with surprise. She moaned, and fabric ripped a second before her fingers thrust into his hair, the tattered remains of her shirt hanging from one arm. "*Seamus.*"

To speak, he'd have to raise his head, and he was nowhere near ready to relinquish the warm taste of her. Not yet.

One heel dug into his back as she squirmed, tugging at his hair in time with her short, gasping moans. "This is—this is so good, so *wicked.*"

He turned his head and bit the inside of her thigh. "Wicked?"

She snarled and tightened her fingers in his hair as power swelled, fierce dominant magic that trembled with her pleasure even as it challenged him.

It was a sweet challenge, and one Seamus couldn't resist. He eased her off the counter and turned her over it. He dropped a single kiss on the smooth line of her spine and held her hips still. "Say yes."

"How many times do I have to say it?" She rocked back, rubbed her ass against his cock with a throaty moan. "This is how I imagined it the first time. This is what she's wanted all along. Give me what I want. Take me."

Something in him told him she meant it, and that something rejoiced as he thrust into her, sinking deep with a groan.

Joan choked on a gasping moan, and he knew her inhibitions had been stripped bare when she reached for his hands and dragged them up, pressing them to her breasts with another desperate noise. "T-touch me, please—"

"Soft?" He plucked at her nipples, teasing them into hard peaks before twisting them just a little. "Or like that?"

"Like that." Her fingernails dragged across his wrists before her hands slammed against the counter, bracing her shaking body.

She tightened around him with every caress, and Seamus steeled himself against release. He couldn't come, not yet. "I know what you need." He cupped her breast, squeezing her nipple between his fingers, and slipped his other hand down the front of her body.

Her body clenched and her head crashed back against his shoulder. "More. Harder."

He bit her ear and gave her the dirty words she wanted. "Not until you come on my cock."

She did, with a sobbing moan of pleasure, her hands slipping against the counter as she tried to rock back against him with the rhythm of her body's frantic release.

He gripped her hips, gritted his teeth against his own need to follow and gave her what she *needed* then—hard, driving thrusts that pushed her against the biting edge of the counter. One of her hands flew out, knocking a vase to the floor. She whimpered and pushed up on her toes as her head fell forward, baring the back of her neck to him save for a few strands of wild hair.

He bit her before he could stop himself, and that jubilant voice inside him whispered that she wouldn't want him to stop. She'd given herself to him, and now...

Now he'd give himself to her. He closed his teeth harder on her neck and drove deep as release took him, pleasure tearing through him in white-hot waves.

When it faded Joan had gone liquid underneath him, her head resting on her folded arms as tiny tremors shivered through her, aftershocks of pleasure he could feel deep inside her. Her breath came in short, gasping pants that slowed gradually, until she found the breath to whisper. "I think I might grow to like being a werewolf."

He laughed and eased back to make sure he wasn't crushing her. "I'm glad I could help."

"I'm glad I let you." One of her hands drifted up to her neck, fingers caressing the spot where he'd bit her. "It's like everything means more. How can one bite feel better than the sex?"

"Because we shared ourselves."

She straightened slowly and nudged him until she had space enough to turn and stare up at him. A smile curved her lips as she reached to brush her fingers through his tousled hair. "Because we fit together."

"Yes." Admitting as much should have caused him more than a moment's worry, but it was too late. Seamus wasn't one to fight his instincts. "And now we should rest."

Joan's smile widened. "Am I so distracting you forgot you were hungry?"

He'd manage without the meal, but she would need the

strength. "Blast it, I had forgotten."

She laughed and tugged at his shirt until he relinquished it, then pulled it over her own head before smoothing her rumpled skirt down. "So we'll cook together. How much of a mess can I make of it?"

He didn't care if they made a mess, as long as it made her smile.

Chapter Six

By the time the seventh day dawned without an attack, Joan was ready to climb out of her skin.

The first few had felt like a joyful reprieve, a chance to rest and prepare, to plan. She'd made her lists, had discussed the strengths and weaknesses of every man Edwin might be able to call to his cause, from the alpha himself straight to the weakest of subordinates.

When she'd run out of words, she'd enjoyed the free time in other ways, ways that made her blush to consider. But the joyous sense of freedom had constricted a little more with each day, until she felt tension as a painful knot between her shoulders. The ax had to fall; there was no way it *couldn't*.

Waiting for it might drive her mad. It did drive her to snap at Seamus as she paced her bedroom, the need to move having driven her from beneath the blankets at the first light of sunrise. "I thought they'd come at once." It wasn't the first time she'd said it, but she didn't care anymore. At least words gave her some release from twisting fear. "What if they're hurting them more, and I've been wasting my time indulging myself. A *week*, and no one could have held Astrid so long. Not without—" A hitching breath as she forced the thought away, tried to deny her sinking surety that her friend was dead. "I should have gone sooner—"

"Then you would have accomplished nothing by rushing in

and getting yourself killed," he reasoned.

She didn't want to hear reason. "Right now nothing I do could be categorized as rushing. They're not going to walk into our trap. Maybe I need to walk into theirs."

"Can't just do it." He sat, the sheets falling to his waist. "If you want to live, we have to be careful."

The claustrophobia of being trapped grated so harshly on her nerves that even the bare, beautiful expanse of his chest couldn't hold her attention for more than a few moments. "I have no skill at this. I don't plan battles. I understand a clean challenge, a fight. I don't understand this."

"If we could know it would be a clean challenge, we'd be gone already." Seamus patted the bed. "Come here."

If she went to the bed he'd lay his hands on her, and her traitorous wolf would be soothed just by his touch. It should frighten her more, how easily he could quiet her panic, but today it only made her angry. She didn't want to be petted and tamed, she wanted to fight. "No. If you have an idea, tell me what it is."

"I'm not trying to distract you." He tilted his head. "Come *here*."

The command held a thrust of power, and she bared her teeth at him. "Don't get alpha with me, Seamus Whelan. Not unless you want to smash me in line with your fists."

His lips trembled as he quite obviously fought a smile. "I'll never rule you, sweet Joan. Only ask. Please."

The plea did what an order couldn't, and she capitulated with a sigh and slid onto the bed next to him. "Don't issue orders when I'm riled up unless you want me to challenge you on principle. I can't help myself."

He looked like he might not be so averse to the occasional challenge. For now, he wrapped an arm around her shoulders.

"I have an idea," he murmured against her shoulder, "and I need your help figuring out if it would work."

Nervous tension bled from her body as her wolf quieted at the gentle brush of his magic. At least it made it easier to think. "What's your idea?"

"It involves two things—the bad blood between Lancaster and the alpha, and a good scratch man I happen to know."

"A scratch man?"

"A scratch man is a forger," he told her, "but not just any forger. The kind who can fool anyone. The kind who can get things done." Seamus stroked his hand down her arm, from shoulder to wrist and back again, over and over. Then he began to speak just as slowly, outlining his plan.

Edwin Lancaster's estate was about what Seamus expected, huge and austere and brimming with the stink of fear. The men milling about were scared of Lancaster, that much was obvious. Should he displace the alpha, he would rule the pack with anger and threats.

It had happened in the past, of course, but that control wouldn't have lasted for long before another would have risen to rid the pack of the tyranny. These days, though...

Money was God.

Seamus held Joan's hand tighter as one of Edwin's guards led them through a small courtyard and toward a large set of French doors. They crashed open, and Lancaster stood there, pleased but also angry. "Joanie."

Joan's fingernails dug painful furrows in Seamus's hand. "I want your assurance that Adam and Gavin and the girls are still safe."

"They're here. They're alive." His gaze flickered to Seamus.

"Mostly."

Distantly, Seamus recognized the anger that raged through him. He tamped it down. "I challenge you for their freedom, for what you've done to them...and for what's yours." He delivered the final words with a smile he knew would infuriate the man.

Edwin's look of shock was almost comical, but when his eyes focused on Seamus and Joan's joined hands, something feral and ugly crept over his expression. "So, the virtuous Miss Fuller is revealed to be a common whore. I hope you got your payment upfront."

Oddly, the ugly words did nothing to further Seamus's ire. It didn't matter what this man thought—a man who, for all his finery and affluence, was more of a thug than Seamus himself had ever been. "I challenge you, Edwin Lancaster. Are you tucking tail and showing your belly in forfeit?"

"No." Disdain dripped from him. "I accept your challenge."

"Excellent." Seamus caught movement out of the corner of his eye as Lancaster's men moved into position, readying for an attack. "What are your terms? Fists? Teeth?"

"I have no interest in exchanging blows like a petty criminal. We fight as wolves are meant to."

"Do we now?" The men moved closer, and Seamus released Joan. "Let's have done with it, then."

Joan might be fairly trembling with rage, but she kept to the plan and stepped back, hands curled into fists at her side. Edwin's eyes narrowed as he reached for the buttons on his vest. "Don't look so upset, little Joan. You're free of me. I don't marry whores and I don't bed cold-hearted bitches."

Her lips curled into a vicious, deadly smile. "Be glad he claimed the right to challenge you. He might kill you quickly."

"Enough," Seamus grated, hoping she would understand. If the plan fell through and Lancaster won, her threats could cost her her life.

Joan glanced at him and then away, fixing her gaze on the ground as she visibly dragged her temper back under control. The sight only amused Lancaster more. He laughed, the sound grating and harsh, and shed his vest. "How touching. Someone finally brought you to heel."

Seamus stripped off his own vest and began to unbutton his shirt. "You're spending an awful lot of time heckling a girl, Lancaster. Don't want to fight me?"

"I'm not afraid of you." The words were pure bluster, undercut by the way his eyes kept flicking from left to right, clearly sizing up his supporters.

"Right." Seamus smiled. "Then why are you waiting for your men to jump me?"

It might have been the truth, but Lancaster's pride couldn't take it. His fingers closed around his crisply pressed shirt and he jerked, sending buttons flying. "Ridiculous."

"Clean," Seamus told him. "A clean fight, or I'll take your fucking head off right here, while you're still tangled up in your pretty clothes."

Lancaster's hands fisted, something sly passing behind his eyes. "You could try."

"Or I could." They'd both been so distracted with the posturing that neither had noticed Samuel's arrival. The Boston alpha stood at the front of the courtyard, his arms crossed over his chest. "Surely you're not thinking of cheating, Edwin? I had to stop you once this week already, that silly business with the wizard."

Behind Seamus, Joan's breath released in a gusty sigh of relief, as if she'd almost believed they'd been betrayed. But as Samuel stared expectantly, the loose circle of men surrounding Seamus and Edwin broke apart.

Edwin wasn't stupid. He looked from Samuel to Joan, angry color rising in his face. "You double-crossing bitch."

Her chin came up. "Only you would think ensuring a fair fight is cheating."

Seamus kicked off his shoes. "Enough. Here and now, Lancaster."

When his opponent didn't reply, Samuel took a step forward. "You're stalling. You've avoided too many challenges of late. Fight now or forfeit."

Edwin's shoulders slumped just the slightest bit, and Seamus knew he knew he'd been defeated already. He would still fight because he had to, but the alpha was finally ready to move against him. To preserve his position.

Then Edwin's eyes gleamed, and he squared his shoulders and spoke again. "This man's problem with me isn't his problem at all. It's hers." He cut his eyes at Joan. "If anyone challenges me, it should be her, should it not?"

She'd grudgingly agreed to cede the challenge to Seamus, but now not even their plan could hold her. "I accept. Now, with the alpha and Seamus standing witness."

Before Seamus could argue, the alpha nodded. "It will stand. Whelan, step back."

He had no choice but to comply, and only the fact that Edwin was a coward and a weakling allowed him to do so without physical restraint. From the way Joan looked at him as she slipped out of her shoes, she understood the cost of his self-control. A tiny, secretive smile played around the edges of her lips as she straightened and whispered, "Thank you."

It eased his hackles somewhat. "I know you threatened to kill him slowly, but I'd appreciate it if you made it quick."

Joan laughed, looking like an entirely different woman than the one he'd first met. Wilder. Freer. She reached for the buttons on the front of her oversized shirt and nodded. "Anything for you, my dear man."

That unfettered confidence let him relax more, and he fell back to stand beside the Boston alpha. "She's going to tear into him."

The man seemed unconcerned. "If he can't defend himself against one little deb, he deserves to go down."

"Yes, doesn't he?" Joan's voice slashed through the air as she shed her shirt. "You made me, Edwin. You bit me, you turned me... You took all those girls, stole their lives and threw them away like trash. Now it's time to pay your debts, and this time your money won't make it go away."

Edwin opened his mouth to deliver a rejoinder, and she kicked off her pants and knelt to shift.

Seamus crossed his arms over his chest. Surprisingly, he was going to enjoy watching Joan fight this fight.

As a wolf Joan could smell the heavy stink of Edwin's fear. He wasn't a man used to fighting. During normal times he would have settled somewhere in the middle of the pack, not a submissive wolf but not dominant. There was no steely strength in him, no fire, none of the seething power that made the world come alive around her.

Then the world they'd known had ended with the stock market's crash, and Edwin's ability to cling to his fortune had given him all the power he needed. No one challenged the man who fed them.

Before now.

It seemed to take forever for Edwin to call the change. His power fluctuated wildly with the pounding of his heart, skittish and fast enough to rouse her instincts. Scared. Weak. Edwin was prey.

He trembled on his paws, his tail dipping down, as if he wanted to tuck it between his legs and submit, ending the challenge. But Joan knew that the man still inside him wouldn't allow it.

He'd always had more pride than sense.

The men had formed a circle again, a loose one this time, marking the boundary of an acceptable challenge. Joan could sense Seamus at her back, a glowing star of power. A hundred times before she'd considered challenging Edwin, but fear had always held her back. Edwin didn't believe in fair fights. His men would have fallen on her like they'd been planning on attacking Seamus.

Not this time. A fair fight. A clean fight, with Seamus protecting her from duplicity. Baring her teeth, she snarled at Edwin and lunged.

He met her at the shoulder with a hard shove. His greater bulk gave him an advantage, but she was used to being smaller than the males. She twisted away easily and nipped at his side, moving faster than he could hope to.

A good thing too, since even Edwin, with his slight build, was stronger. He could snap his jaws on her throat, so she had to make sure he didn't get the chance.

She had to bring him down.

Edwin wasn't an experienced fighter, but he was desperate. Joan was still considering the best tactic when he came at her, lips pulled back in a vicious snarl. The move held no subtlety, just rage and aggression, but even so his teeth grazed her fur as she twisted away, almost too slow.

No time to think. Instinct took over and she went low this time, driving underneath his guard. Her jaw snapped shut on his back leg. His yelp turned into a howl of pain, but he cut it short and retaliated, biting into her haunch.

Pain sliced through her, intensifying as she endured it long enough to bite again, this time hard enough to snap bone. He went down, but his teeth ripped free of her flesh as he did, rending it in a burning blaze of agony.

Instinct screamed to press the advantage, to ignore her pain and end him before he could hurt anyone else. Instead she hesitated, giving him a chance to yield.

He scrambled up, spittle flying from his jaws as he dove for her throat.

On three legs the attack was clumsy, and part of her had known he couldn't give in. Not to her. She feinted back, let him think she was more injured than she was. That she was scared, intimidated...all the things he wanted to believe.

A perfect trap for his ego, and he tumbled into it, pressing his advantage without a care for defense. She narrowly wrenched her body out of the way of a stumbling attack, then let her leg give out, as if the pain from her left flank was too much.

He shouldn't have believed it. Even a weaker wolf would have recovered from her injury by now, but males always believed females were inferior. Edwin lunged, reckless and triumphant, and Joan twisted at the last moment and closed her jaws around his vulnerable throat.

She'd killed before, when necessity called for it. Her human mind might shy away, but the wolf knew what to do.

Bite.

Tear.

Blood gushed, hot and sharply metallic, and relief swelled as she staggered away, her wolf already secure in their victory.

Edwin toppled, slumped to the ground in a quiet, awkward heap. Blood pooled underneath him and seeped into his meticulously kept lawn. Brutal death amidst the trappings of civilization.

No one spoke. No one *breathed*, not until Seamus finally broke the leash of his control and ran forward to kneel beside her, his hands gently ruffling her fur. "Joan. Are you all right?"

The words drifted over her, more tone than substance. Some part of her knew their meaning, felt the sweet possessiveness in his touch. She should turn, reassure him somehow.

She should celebrate, howl her victory loud enough that the wolves who belonged to her would hear and know themselves safe. The enemy of her nightmares had been brought low. By her.

He was dead. Edwin Lancaster, the man who'd torn her from her family and her life when she'd rejected him. The man who'd thrust her into this nightmarish world of brutality and savagery. Joan stared, her heightened senses filled with the scent of cooling blood.

Dead.

She was free.

Frigid numbness faded under a rush of giddy, reckless excitement. There'd been a time when she'd imagined not even his death would save them. So many wolves had embraced the corruption Edwin fostered. Impossible to imagine the same wasn't happening all across the country, where desperation met money.

No place to run. No place to take the girls whose lives Edwin had destroyed.

Not until Seamus.

He whispered her name again, hands still sliding over her back, questing for injuries. He was worried. Protective. It snapped her out of her shock, and she shook herself and danced away, needing the space to shift.

The agony of the change intensified with a still-healing wound, but Joan pushed through it until she knelt on the blood-slicked ground, her hip throbbing in protest. "My shirt?"

Seamus wrapped his own around her, engulfing her in his warmth and scent. "Do you need a doctor?"

"No." Her fingers trembled as she tangled them in the shirt and clutched it tight around her. She lifted her gaze and found the loose circle of men watching her, their expressions ranging from fury to satisfaction.

Only one man's face was blank—the one man who could betray them yet. "Samuel."

Slowly, the Boston alpha began to smile. "I've done my part."

Seamus nodded. "Yes, you have."

"I trust you haven't forgotten our agreement." Samuel's expression darkened. "If you don't hold up your end of the deal, I could still make life very difficult for Miss Fuller and—"

Seamus held up a hand to stop his words. "I know someone who can transfer Lancaster's assets to the pack. I'll contact him immediately."

"Then I believe everyone will agree that Edwin decided to take an extended trip. A tour of Europe, perhaps?"

Joan closed her eyes and took a steadying breath. "My people."

"In the guest house. Edwin kept them there, under guard."

The answer didn't soothe her. "He couldn't have kept Adam and Gavin in check with a guard."

Samuel looked away. "Edwin always has—had his ways."

Which meant some of them had died to keep the men in line. Ice slipped through her veins, and it took all of the stubborn pride she possessed to lift herself to her feet. Her leg wouldn't quite hold her yet, but Seamus was quick enough to offer support. "I'm taking them with me, Samuel. We're leaving Boston."

"That was part of the deal."

"A part we're keeping," Seamus whispered, close to her ear.

Joan nodded and tightened her fingers around his hand. "I'd like to see them while you and Seamus discuss your business."

The alpha shook his head. "Business will keep. Take her to see them, and we'll talk later."

Seamus slid his arm around her waist and nearly lifted her off her feet. "Come on. I'll help you."

In times past she never would have accepted his assistance. She would have swallowed pain and accepted the misery of appearing uninjured. Many of the men who watched their slow progress across the uneven ground had been enemies. To show weakness, to be vulnerable in front of them— it would have invited challenge.

With Seamus at her side she didn't have to be strong every moment of every day. She could curl her arm around his neck and let him help her. So she did, shaking a little as she hooked her arm over his shoulder. "For a second I thought you wouldn't let me fight him."

A flash of guilt skated across his face. "I almost didn't."

"I know." She smiled a little, in spite of everything. "I won't blame you for your instincts, as long as you try to fight them once in a while."

"And I held back," he allowed. "Even when the son of a bitch bit you."

"I'm strong enough to fight when I have to, Seamus. But knowing you're at my back...it means everything."

"I will be, sweet Joan." His eyes blazed with intensity. "Your fights are mine, and mine are yours."

The words rocked through her, wiping away pain and fear in a rush of relief that weakened her knees. "That means your people are mine, and mine are yours."

"Thought we'd settled that already, love."

"I suppose we did." She hesitated in front of the door to the guesthouse, then squared her shoulders. Whatever she found on the other side, whatever pain or grief waited, she wouldn't have to face it alone.

She'd never have to face anything alone again. "Let's see to our people."

Seamus pushed open the door, and at first she could only see the faces of the missing. Opal, whose death she had all but ordered through ruthless practicality. Astrid, their witch, who she'd known in her heart must be gone because Astrid could never be held captive, not for so long. Not when the first person to lay an ungentle hand on Maggie would have had to kill her or forfeit his own life.

A more ruthless leader might have considered it a triumph. Not so many were missing. Opal, Astrid, a young, quiet woman named Jasmine and the only male Edwin had captured, a gruff older wolf who'd only joined Joan's pack recently. Not so many, but still *too* many. Enough to make victory more bitter than sweet, and Joan ached for every life as if every death had been hers alone to prevent.

Seamus's arm slid around her waist again, a comforting strength. "Joan?"

She swallowed and pulled herself together. For them. "We're leaving. We've found a safe place, and everyone else is already on the way there."

A quiet, pained noise filled the air, and two of the girls moved, giving Joan her first glimpse of Adam stretched out on an immaculately upholstered sofa. He was pale, as pale as human legends so often painted vampires, and even sitting upright seemed a struggle, though he flinched away from the one girl who reached out to help him.

Dull, tired eyes focused on her waist, on Seamus's arm around her and the unspoken statement inherent in the gesture. When Adam's gaze lifted to hers, he looked almost relieved. "You don't need me anymore."

Seamus glanced around, his mouth open as if to speak. Before he could, Gavin shouldered out of the small crowd with a grimace. "Whelan."

"Gavin." His relief was palpable.

But his friend paused only for a brief greeting before turning to Joan. "Talk some sense into Adam. He's half-killed himself trying to help everyone, but he won't feed."

Joan slipped away from Seamus and moved to stand in front of the sofa, her throat tight with tears she still couldn't shed. Wouldn't shed—not yet. "Adam."

The vampire looked away. "I'm leaving, Joan. Gavin's going to help Seamus get everyone to safety. Wolves helping wolves. That's how it should be."

She hadn't always approved of Adam. Sometimes she hadn't even liked him very much, but she'd always respected him. Appreciated him. "You helped us. For years, you helped us. Let us help you now."

"No." His eyes closed. "The bonds are gone. Astrid's gone. I need to go too. I need some time." His fists clenched on his legs. "Do you really want to look at me, day in and day out, and see the ghosts?"

As if the ghosts wouldn't follow him wherever he went, just like they'd follow her. "We always see them. They deserve to be seen. And Astrid—" She glanced at Maggie, curled in the corner between the protective press of two of her friends, her eyes red and swollen, her expression numb.

Adam didn't turn his head, but he seemed to know where her gaze had wandered. "Take care of her. For Astrid. For me."

Unwavering finality. She could argue, but Adam was unmovable when he set his mind on something. Only Astrid had ever been able to sway him. "I will," she whispered. "We'll take care of all of them. Gavin will know where we are. If you need a safe place..."

"Take care, Joan." Adam finally looked at her, just for a moment, and she saw a world of loneliness and loss and something that went beyond both, a soul-deep envy that sharpened as he looked past her again. "Let him love you, Joanie."

"We just met, Adam. It's not—" The words wouldn't come, because she knew they weren't true. Love bloomed over a lifetime of days, but it could kindle in a moment. In the space between heartbeats, with something as small as a promise— *Your fights are mine, and mine are yours.*

The tiniest smile curved Adam's lips when she didn't finish her denial. "You never were stupid."

"No, I suppose I wasn't." She hesitated before lowering her voice. "I hope you'll let someone love you someday."

"Someday," he agreed, but his pleasant tone couldn't cover the lie. Her heart broke a little, but she pasted on a smile and pretended she believed him. She pretended as Gavin and Seamus helped her gather up the girls, pretended as Adam said his awkward goodbyes and someone brought her clothes and pointed her to the bathroom.

She pretended until the door closed behind her, and then she gave in and cried. Silently, because she couldn't afford to alarm the young women who had already been through so much, but the tears burned as she scrubbed at her skin with a wet rag. Another sink in another house and she was still covered with blood and tired of fighting—

But not alone, not this time. The door cracked open and Seamus slipped inside. He watched her in the mirror for a moment before taking the damp cloth and stroking it over her arms. "Dubois left."

Joan closed her eyes and let him take care of her, needing the quiet, steadying support. "I know. I think he's broken inside."

"He did the best he could." Seamus's fingers stroked through her hair. "We all did."

She turned blindly and found him there, arms open and strong as she wrapped herself in his scent and his power and everything that was *Seamus*. "I want to go home. I want to have a home to go to."

"Breckenridge Island?" he whispered against her temple.

It was more primal. More basic. "You."

A soft growl vibrated under her cheek. "You'll always have that, whether we're out there on that island or back in the city. I promise."

She clung to him until she thought his shoulders might bear bruises from her fingers, and even that evoked an instinctive satisfaction. Marked. Hers. "I think my wolf is a little in love with you."

He made a low noise of pleasure. "What we need to do now is see if the rest of you is going to join her."

"When." Joan kissed his cheek, the line of his jaw and then his chin. "Not if. When. I only hope you're not far behind me."

He cupped her face, tilted it up to his. "No," he whispered, somehow making the word sound like an endearment. "Not far at all, love."

The day was chilly, but Seamus had long since discarded his shirt as he worked on fashioning a door for the most recently completed cabin. It would be shared by several of the women, including Elise and her new baby, so they'd worked on making the structure especially sound.

He paused and straightened as he wiped the sweat from his forehead. The settlement was larger already than they'd expected it to be, but word of their defection from the city packs had already spread. More showed up every few days and, soon, overpopulation would cause problems. Not with money—there was plenty of that—but even money couldn't buy shelter or food on this island.

Victor balanced precariously on the steeply slanted roof above him, working on the slate shingles. "How's the door coming?"

"Almost done." It was solid, sound, and it would serve them well through the impending winter. "Not much time left."

"Wind's got a fearsome bite to it. It'll snow any day now. Some of the men may be taking it in shifts bedding down in the barn as wolves, but we'll get through."

Yes, they would. "Remind me to check the coal stores again. You might have to make one last trip into Searsport."

Victor groaned. "That woman has been after me to take her along. Says men don't know how to shop for the things a woman needs."

That had to be Simone. Seamus grinned and settled the finished door against the side of the cabin. "Better listen to her. I get the feeling she doesn't give up easily."

"She's already gone and whined to your mate, and I got that look this morning." Victor's eyebrows pulled together as he slid down the roof and hopped to the ground. "Not telling you how to manage your woman or anything, but shouldn't a newly mated wolf be less crabby?"

"With you? No."

"Damn." Victor tossed his hammer onto the makeshift table and took a step back. "Well, we've got that order coming in from Boston in a few weeks. And there's a lot of work to do here, still. No time to take two trips, so she'll just have to wait."

"Simone will manage." Seamus stretched and slid his arms into his shirt. "Joan's expecting me for lunch. Something special, she said, and keep your mind out of the gutter."

"Mm-hmm." Victor didn't take his gaze from the house. "This is going to be a long winter, Whelan."

"A hard winter." There was no use sugarcoating that particular fact. "We'll all have to work, no doubt about it."

"It could be years before we can get reliable electricity going out here. How many of these girls want to live like this? They're soft. City girls." Victor's jaw tightened. "Christ, they're scared."

Their fear had to be eating at Victor, just as it was at him. But at least he had Joan to soothe him. "We've got money, Vic, and that makes things happen. It'll be faster than you think, we just have to keep it together until then."

"I know." Victor sighed and ran a hand through his disheveled hair. "Go. See your woman. And ask her to keep her friend from pestering me. That one hasn't got a scared bone in her body."

"Right." Even Victor's grumpiness couldn't disguise the fact that he admired Simone's fearlessness. "Watch yourself. She's got a beau. One who could turn you into a frog, come to think of it."

"Ain't afraid of any wizard."

Most of the others didn't feel that way. The magic at the wizard's command was strong, and beyond most of the wolves' understanding, including his own. That sort of magic could confine him, or compel him to act against his own desires or conscience—and that was terrifying.

But in this first year, when their tiny island still lacked for so many comforts and amenities, magic could prove invaluable. "We need him here in case something goes wrong. He's a skilled healer."

"Yeah, yeah. I'm not arguing. If I live another hundred years, I hope I never have to deliver a baby in the backseat of a car again."

"With luck, you shouldn't have to." Seamus raised a hand in farewell. "I'll tell Joan you said hello, and please keep Simone the hell away from you."

Victor turned back to the house and picked up his hammer. "I'm gonna finish up here. See you later, Whelan."

A short walk brought Seamus to his own door. Given a choice, he'd have preferred privacy, to be set away from the others a bit, but for the sake of safety and convenience, they all needed to stick close together.

Especially the alphas. When he opened the door, the scent of blueberry pie greeted him. "Smells good."

"Because Mary was here. All I have to do is manage not to burn it." Joan had a patchwork apron tied over her jeans and thick sweater, and the sight of her bent over the table made his mouth water. "But Guy brought in his first haul from the traps today. And he showed me how to cook them. I think."

"Good, lobster for dinner." He caught the ties of her apron and spun her around to land in his arms. "Good afternoon, Miss Fuller."

She laughed, happiness brightening her face. "Mr. Whelan, your obsession with ambushing me in the kitchen is becoming its own vice."

"I gave up all my others. You're the only one I have left, sweet Joan, and I intend to indulge." Especially over the long, cold nights ahead.

Her fingers traced along his jaw as her eyes softened into the look she never wore for anyone else, the one that said more clearly than words that she was his lover, his mate. His. "Well, fancy that. I've redeemed your criminal heart. Of course, you've turned me into a shameless wanton who might very well have her way with you in broad daylight on the kitchen table."

"Mmm." He lifted her and set her down on the edge of the aforementioned table, urging her legs around his waist as he moved. "I could get used to it, but your aprons might start to excite me."

Joan landed a playful nip on his chin, but when she leaned forward to wrap her arms around him and bury her face against his neck, it became clear she was more interested in cuddling than sex. "Victor said to expect a blizzard soon. I admit, I'm almost a little relieved. We've been so busy getting ready, some days it seems like the only time we get to spend together is while we're sleeping."

"We're as ready as we can be." He was looking forward to it too—no one in the white, whirling world except for them. "Nothing we can't handle if we work together, right?"

"Nothing at all." Her breath tickled against his neck, warm and teasing. The soft words that followed, however, were deadly earnest. "I love you. More every day."

Three tiny words, but they never failed to move him. His chest tightened, and he cradled her closer. "And I love you."

"I'm so lucky to have you. After everything—" Her voice hitched, and her fingers dug hard against his shoulders. "But we've done it. We made a safe place. A sanctuary."

"Yes." He knew only one dark spot remained, sullying her happiness. "I wish we could have convinced Adam to stay here this winter."

"We couldn't. Not without Astrid...she was his contemporary. I was... We were never close. Not like that."

"Then he'll need time." There was nothing they could do to help him heal, not if they only served as painful reminders of the deaths of those under his charge.

"We all need time." She pulled back and lifted her hands, cradling his face with a gentle smile. "Now we have it."

"There's my smile." He traced his thumb over her lower lip. "Blueberry pie. Is that my surprise?"

Joan twisted in his arms and reached behind her, turning back to him with a rich-looking leather-bound book cradled between her hands. "It's not much, but I thought we needed at least one book in our library before the blizzards start."

Only Joan would have known that being stuck without something to read would vex him more than any other amenity the island lacked, and the knowledge filled him with a warming satisfaction. "I love Whitman," he told her as he set the book aside, "but nowhere near as much as I love you."

"I expect you to spend the long winter nights reading me poetry now, you know."

"I'd be happy to." Happier than she knew, but that was all right. He had time to show her. "I'll read it in bed. Wanna try it out?"

Joan laughed, all traces of grief vanished in a joyful rush of power and pleasure. "The pie will burn." She didn't sound like she cared.

"It'll be fine." The pie, like just about everything else, could wait, but his need for Joan was paramount. Overwhelming.

Overwhelming because it was a need borne of affection as well as lust. He could talk to her, share things with her.

She arched an eyebrow. "You're staring."

114

"I'm looking."

"Looking at what?"

That answer was simple. "My love." Joan was his partner, a true mate, and he would never turn back.

Undertow

Dedication

Dedicated to Alisha Rai, Keith Melton and Vivian Arend, three amazing authors with amazing hearts, who know when to laugh, when to yell, and when to start a fake Twitter feud just to brighten an otherwise gloomy day.

Chapter One

Victor hated lobsters.

A month ago he hadn't given a damn about the things. They were decent enough eating when someone set one in front of him already cooked, but those days of leisure were long past.

Now he was on a boat. A boat that reeked of rotting fish, engine fuel and brine. Bad for a human nose but torment to his werewolf senses. Not even the cold could numb the unpleasant odor as Victor slammed the cover onto the bait container. "Does this have to smell so damn bad?"

"The lobsters like it," Guy answered matter-of-factly. The smell didn't seem to bother him, though Victor imagined no one would know if it did.

Victor bit back his instinctive response—*Fuck the lobsters*—and pounded his fist on the cover of the bait container once, just to make sure it was tight. At least the day's haul was respectable. In the month the pack had been on the island, they'd been scrambling to get traps into the waters Guy's family had fished for generations.

It wasn't much, but it was food. By the end of winter, Victor imagined they'd all be tired of clams, lobster and venison, but with their tiny little island overrun with deer and surrounded by prime fishing water...

Well, these days you ate what you could get.

Victor shifted his attention to the crate of lobsters as Guy steered the boat toward the island's only dock, a rickety old wooden walkway extending a good twenty feet into the ocean before ending in a floating platform. When spring rolled around, they'd have to rebuild it, and they'd certainly need to make it more permanent, but for now it served as an easy way to unload their catch.

They were still a hundred feet from the dock when two figures emerged from the path that led up into the twisting trees. Thick coats, scarves and hats obscured shape and features, but even at this distance Victor's body tensed in recognition. He'd agreed to spend his days on Guy's boat to get away from her, judging the rough work better than the uncomfortable way Simone scraped his control into tatters with only her presence.

"There's an easier way." He barely heard Guy's voice over the rumble of the motor. "Ask her to leave you alone."

The curse of spending too long with the same companions was their unappealing ability to understand those things left unspoken. Though if anyone had to pry into his business, he supposed it might as well be Guy. Of all the men he'd worked alongside for so many years, Guy was the one who understood him best. He was the only other man who'd been born a werewolf, who'd lived with the same twisting instincts every day of his life.

Victor jerked his gaze from the shoreline and studied the dock instead. "I can't."

"Can't or won't?"

"Can't," he replied, lowering his voice. Sound carried so easily on the water, and Simone had a werewolf's hearing, after all. "Her instincts bring her back, even when I push her away. I don't have it in me to push hard enough to crush that. It would hurt her."

Guy snorted. "I think it's better to have done with it. She'll be fine."

Yes, her wizard beau would comfort her. Victor's fists tightened until his knuckles ached, but there was no fight to be had. His instinctive distrust of witches aside, he couldn't attack the only healer on their island just because his pride stung. "Stay out of it, Guy. It's not your business."

"Maybe not, but still." Guy lifted a hand in greeting, and the two women returned his wave. "Don't know much, but I know any woman would be mortified to discover she'd been making a fool of herself over a man."

Victor turned and leveled an unfriendly look at Guy. "That woman has a suitor. She's not interested in me. And when things settle down and these girls know they're safe from the corrupt packs, her wolf won't be interested either. So let it lie."

Guy met his glare with a mild look. "What if you're wrong?"

Then maybe he'd find some relief from long lonely nights bedded down in the only privacy the island offered—the tiny cabin on his sailboat. "Make up your damn mind. Should I tell her to leave me alone or try to stake a claim on a taken woman?"

One dark eyebrow shot up. "I wasn't aware you wanted to claim her. I was just saying a little blunt honesty is better than leading a lady on."

Shit. "I said to let it lie." They'd pulled close enough to the dock that further conversation was inadvisable, so Victor turned and raised his hand as well. The figures were more distinct now, clear enough that Victor recognized Simone's companion—Rose, a quiet, serious young woman who seemed capable of passing endless hours in total silence.

The two women had piled buoys on the dock, the paint so fresh he could smell it at a distance. "We heard the boat and decided to come down!" Simone called as Guy killed the

121

outboard engine.

Victor climbed up on the side of the boat and made the hop to the dock as soon as they were close enough. "Got through all the buoys today?" Inane small talk, but it served as something to say as he waited for Guy to throw him a rope.

"These are from yesterday," she told him, nudging one with her boot. "The ones we painted today are hung up near the shed."

Because the paint hadn't dried yet, something he would have figured out if he'd bothered to think about it. Victor caught the rope Guy tossed toward the dock and waited for the other man to flip the bumpers over the railing before pulling the small skiff snug against the dock.

The now-familiar task left too much room to dwell on the way Simone's presence prickled along his skin. She wasn't a very powerful werewolf, but she had a gentle strength that soothed the wildest parts of him. Acrid paint covered most of her scent, but underneath he caught the hint of lilacs, a subtle smell that had begun to stir his body every time she approached.

Guy nodded to the women as he lifted the crate containing the day's catch. "Have either of you ladies seen Seamus and Joan? I've got a few ideas to run by them before the meeting tonight."

"They should be home. Joan said they're going to spend the afternoon going over the supply lists they gathered."

Which meant the alpha was planning to spend the afternoon making love to his new mate. Joan might still be the same prickly little alpha bitch who could shrivel a man's balls with a look, but Seamus, at least, seemed to be benefiting from whatever sexual escapades went on behind locked doors. Victor hadn't seen his old friend so content with life in decades, a fact that made his own suffering that much sharper.

Rose spoke up for the first time, her soft voice barely carrying over the lap of the waves and the creaking of the dock. "It might be best not to disturb them."

Guy's dark eyes twinkled, and he smiled at Rose. "I think you might be right."

The girl's cheeks were already pink from the biting wind, but Victor thought he saw a hint of a blush before Rose smiled shyly. "It's my turn to manage dinner for the workers. I hoped I could collect some of the catch and get an early start?"

"Right here." Guy jumped down to the dock with the crate. "I'll walk with you."

Simone waved at their retreating backs, a rueful expression on her face. "He's left you to deal with me *and* the boat. Which is a more daunting prospect?"

He wasn't entirely sure. "I think he's just sweet on Rose."

"You didn't answer my question." She winked at him. "But I'll overlook it, just this once, if you'll tell me when you plan to leave for Searsport."

The trip was a week overdue, but the first blizzard of the season had made it smarter to stick close to the island. "Tomorrow or the day after, probably. You still determined to come?"

"Yes." She flashed him a brilliant, already familiar smile.

Too damn charming—and not real. Oh, she was cheerful all right, the most aggressively optimistic person he'd ever laid eyes on, but she only laid it on thick when she thought someone needed encouragement—or to be worked around to her way of thinking.

Victor quirked one eyebrow. "Still trying your smiles on me?"

Her grin faded into a soft chuckle. "You're the only one who doesn't fall for it."

So she thought. That damn smile tugged at him every time she leveled it. "I should think you could toss a few more of them at your wizard and he'd magic you a boat out of thin air."

Simone looked away, out over the water. "James isn't *my* wizard."

His wolf agreed, more than he could allow. Victor squashed that feral curiosity and kept his voice quiet. Gentle. "He hasn't done anything inappropriate, has he?"

Her gaze snapped back to his face, disbelief clear in her widened eyes. "What? No. He's a very decent man."

He's a wizard. Not a bias he could speak aloud, not when they owed the man too much. "Of course."

She studied his face, somehow seeing what he didn't say, and frowned. "James has sacrificed a lot to help us this winter."

"I know." He curled the rope from the boat around his hand tight enough to bite into his skin and let the pain distract him. "We all have our pasts. And wizards go bad too."

An unexpected sympathy colored her eyes, but she blinked and it was gone. "I'll let you get back to your work. Will you be at the meeting tonight?"

"Of course." Victor stepped up onto the side of the boat, mostly to get away from her before he gave in to temptation and moved closer. "You'd best go rescue Rose. Guy thinks he's more charming than he is."

"Don't we all?" she asked breezily. She took a step back and then turned toward the shore, her hands shoved in her coat pockets, shoulders hunched against the chilly wind.

He'd hurt her. In protecting himself he'd hurt her instead, and his feet landed on the floating dock before he realized he'd moved. He looped the rope around one of the cleats and tied it off in a sloppy knot, then caught up with Simone and touched her shoulder. "I'm sorry."

She barely paused. "You have nothing to apologize for, Victor. I'll see you later."

He wanted to stop her. Touch her. Hold her. She wanted to leave. Victor had never had it in him to cage a woman who so clearly wanted to escape. "Have a good afternoon, Simone."

"You too." She hurried up the path, practically running now, and disappeared into the thick trees at the top of the rise, leaving Victor alone with a boat and an aching emptiness in his chest.

Chapter Two

The fish stew was thick and savory—one of her better efforts, thanks to Rose's tutelage—but Simone laid her spoon beside her bowl anyway. "I suppose I'm not very hungry tonight, after all."

James put down his spoon as well, a hint of worry in his eyes. "Has it been a long day, then?"

"A little tiring." She dropped her hands to her lap and curled them into fists. Her pale skin bore calluses now, rough and unattractive, but she figured they were better than the blisters she'd suffered the first few weeks.

They'd been on Breckenridge Island for a month, and they'd all worked hard to ensure everyone would make it through the coming winter, safe and healthy. In some ways, she'd been unprepared for the harshness of life on the tiny coastal island. In others, it had been a dream.

A dream marred only by the vague sense of disquiet she couldn't seem to shake, the feeling that their idyllic retreat was an illusion, and there was a trap still waiting to spring shut on her.

She smiled anyway, more out of habit than anything else. "Don't fret, James. I'm fine. Everything is fine."

For once, he didn't smile in return. "If that were true, you wouldn't have to spend so much time telling me it's so. You don't need to be fine, Simone. Simply be honest."

"I'm worried about the preparations we've made," she admitted finally. "Or, more specifically, the ones for which we've had no time."

"We're not completely cut off," James pointed out carefully. "Trips to the mainland won't be fun. But we'll get by."

An uncharitable voice in her whispered that James couldn't possibly know what it was like to feel so acutely responsible for the lives of those weaker than oneself. She immediately felt terrible, because of course he did. He was their healer, the closest thing they had to a doctor. *Everyone's* lives potentially rested on his shoulders.

She reached across the small, rough-hewn table and covered his hand with hers. "You always know how to restore my optimism."

He twisted his wrist and clasped her fingers, rubbing his thumb across her knuckles in a whisper-soft caress. The magic inside him was different than her own, but it still pulsed gently whenever their skin touched. "I'd rather give you a bit of time when you don't need to be optimistic."

She lifted the teapot with her free hand and refilled his cup. "And what would that accomplish?"

"Don't you grow weary of it?"

Sometimes she did tire of the expectation that she would always be cheerful, always bolster everyone's morale, but she never put on an act. "If I feel less than chipper, I don't pretend otherwise, James. I don't wear an impenetrable, smiling mask under which I shed sad tears."

He slipped his hand from hers and sat back. "I can't tell as easily as a wolf could."

Simone couldn't blame him for assuming his humanity to be the cause for the lingering distance between them. "I'm sorry, I didn't mean to be flippant. Your only concern is for my happiness."

"Be flippant if it pleases you. We're friends, first and foremost. Always." His hair spilled over his forehead, and he didn't push it back. "You know that, don't you?"

"Yes." A smile curved her lips. "And I'm glad to have a friend like you."

The smile he offered her in return was gentle and warm, but it evoked nothing more than easy companionship. Her heart didn't pound, and her breath didn't catch. "You know I hope to be more someday," he said, "but we have time. I'm happy to be your friend for now."

For now. She'd already begun to suspect that no amount of time would stir her heart beyond friendship—or her body to desire his. Not when a single look from Victor already did both.

Don't you dare, Simone. It was unforgivable to think of another while she sat with James, especially a man like Victor, quiet and severe, who took pains to avoid her at every opportunity and couldn't hide his discomfort at her attention.

A smart woman would have taken the hint already, but she couldn't seem to stop herself from seeking him out. At first, she'd thought perhaps he only needed time to get to know her— but, if anything, time had served only to increase his dislike of her.

"Simone." Worry laced James's voice. "I didn't mean I wouldn't still be your friend if that's all you want from me. It came out wrong."

"I understood what you meant." And, since there was nothing more to say, she changed the subject. "I'm going to Searsport. Tomorrow, or perhaps Thursday."

This time there was no mistaking the tension in his eyes. "With Victor."

"Yes, despite his best efforts." She lifted her cup with a surprisingly steady hand. "Rest easy, James. He's done everything but forbid me to accompany him."

He blew out an exasperated breath. "And why should it make me rest easy to know that he's treating you unkindly? If this is a wolf thing, it's beyond my understanding."

"He isn't—" Simone bit her lip. Most of the time, Victor treated her with polite distance. Even when he lost his patience and snapped at her, he was careful to apologize. "He isn't unkind."

"If bringing you to the mainland is such a trial for Victor, why don't you wait until Guy has a free day? He can't haul lobsters *every* day."

So far, that hadn't been the case. Guy had been out on his boat every morning at dawn, hauling and resetting traps. "I can ask, see if he has some time."

Awkward silence filled the space between them, until James picked up his spoon. "The soup is very good. One of Rose's recipes?"

"Rose doesn't use recipes, much to my chagrin. She just *cooks.*"

"She's good at it." He took another taste, then deftly steered the conversation toward safer ground. "How are the reading lessons going?"

James was one of the few people who knew exactly why she'd been spending so much time with Rose. "Very well. All she needed was for someone to acquaint her with the basics."

"I'm sure. She seems like a smart girl."

"She is." Just another of Edwin's later conquests, when he'd moved beyond concerning himself with the illusion of propriety. When he'd developed a taste for desperation.

Simone had seen dozens of them come through Edwin's

bedroom, poor girls with no prospects. Some had been dazzled by his wealth in the face of the Depression gripping the rest of the country, or even dazzled by *him*, by his smooth charm and pleasant looks. But others, like Rose, had known exactly what they'd get out of serving Edwin in bed. All things considered, she was one of the lucky ones. She hadn't had her heart broken.

James slid his hand over hers, comforting this time, and proved he knew her well enough to guess the path of her thoughts. "He's gone."

His words startled her. "I'm not—I was never scared of Edwin. Not for myself."

"Isn't that almost worse? Being scared for others?"

Simone smiled over her teacup. "Perhaps you understand wolves better than you think."

He laughed and shook his head. "Just you. As much as I can, in any case."

"I'm not an enigma." She shrugged. "I'm a simple woman, really."

"Then perhaps I'm a dense man."

"Never." He was lovely, and another swell of guilt rose in Simone. Even if he claimed to have hopes for the future, not expectations, it would be cruel to let those hopes linger. "James..."

He changed the subject again, this time with a forced smile. "I received a message from England in the last batch of correspondence from the mainland. I've been waiting for a good time to tell you, but I suppose I had to think about it first. It's shocking, really. Do you know the wizards and wolves in England have reached a tentative truce?"

She was glad she'd already lowered her cup, or she might have dropped it. "They've been at war for centuries."

"I know." A smile played about the corners of his lips. "A fondness for werewolves must run in my family. My uncle is heavily involved in the negotiations, and one of my cousins as well. They've been asking me to join them, as I have some understanding of the benefits of an alliance."

Her chair fell back as she rose to round the table and throw her arms around his neck. "James, that's wonderful!"

His arms came around her, steady and warm. "I've already told Joan and Seamus. I'm leaving in the spring. I hadn't mentioned it before because...I want you to go with me."

She'd suspected that, if their relationship deepened, he would want her with him when he left, but she'd never imagined it would be for such a reason. To accomplish such things.

Then Victor's face flashed through her mind, his lips set in a firm frown. "I don't know if I can. They might need me here."

"They'll need you this winter." James's hand settled at the small of her back. "You make them feel safe, make them believe that the hard times will pass. And the hard times *will* pass, here."

"But not magically, once winter lifts. Spring will be harder, in some ways."

"Perhaps," he acknowledged quietly. "Though I asked you for reasons not entirely selfish."

What could those possibly be? She bit back the question. "Why, then?"

He leaned back. "Things are dire in Europe. They're building a sort of...refugee community. Wizards and wolves who can't fight anymore. Who want to try to live together."

Simone pulled her chair around the edge of the table and sat. "To set an example?"

"To prove it can be done." James nodded to her. "You're

proof. *We're* proof."

"Breckenridge Island, you mean?"

"And what you were doing out at Adam's," he murmured. "Wolves, a vampire...and a witch."

Realization dawned. "You're talking about Astrid."

"Yes." He brushed her hair back from her face with gentle fingers. "Her father is the senior wizard involved. While he didn't exactly approve of what she was doing here, they corresponded. She often wrote to him, telling him about her friends and her activities."

Astrid had been a dear friend, a cheerful girl whose ready smile had hidden a core of strength on which they'd often relied. "She told him about me?"

"About your gift."

"Astrid told him I had a gift?"

His hand grazed the side of her neck and withdrew. "The way you make people feel at ease. It's not a trait Gunnar— Astrid's father—had ever associated with wolves, and it intrigues him."

"It's not magic, James. Not like what you do. It's just about...talking to people."

"Sometimes that's a magic all its own."

Even if the wizard had only asked for her because of her connection to his dead daughter, her treasured friend, there was still much she could do. "I don't know."

"It isn't important that you decide now. Think about it. And if your people still need you in the spring..." He shook his head. "I couldn't have come to care for you so quickly if you were the sort of woman who would abandon those depending on her."

The complimentary words were enough to make her squirm with conscience. He looked as if he knew her reasons went beyond those she was willing to share, but he didn't push.

Perhaps he's afraid of what you might say. It made sense—too much sense. After all, wasn't that exactly why she had yet to press the issue with Victor?

Suspecting that you were unwanted was not quite the same as knowing for certain.

The only thing Victor hated more than lobsters were the meetings.

The alphas had instituted them as a way to bring everyone together in the one building large enough to hold them all, a sturdy but unadorned structure filled with rough tables and benches that managed to be less comfortable than sitting on the ground. Gathered together, their pack numbered nearly sixty, five times the number they'd planned for when Seamus had originally proposed laying low on the island. The weight of so many wolves crammed into such a small space was enough to make magic crackle through the air in damn near visible arcs.

Sixty werewolves, and over half of them were women. Girls, in some cases, wide-eyed and frightened and totally out of their depth in the uncivilized wilds of Maine. Some of them had been abused, some brutalized. Some were just city girls who'd never known life without electricity and the creature comforts it provided. Victor supposed that made the evening gatherings important. None of these refugees knew about pack and protection, and their new alpha had every intention of teaching them that safety came with submission—and responsibility with dominance.

The knowledge that it was important didn't make the battering press of their terror any easier on Victor's nerves.

Simone was the bright spot. As an alpha, Joan did all right, but Seamus's mate was steely determination and reassuring strength, not warmth and comfort. Simone was the one who drifted through the crowd as the meeting broke up, knowing somehow when to hug and when to smile, knowing who needed an encouraging pep talk or a scolding or just a few friendly words. Joan and Seamus might be building a sanctuary, but Simone was the heart.

"Simone asked Guy to take her to Searsport." Seamus spoke casually, and a quick glance at his alpha's face told Victor he'd been caught staring.

He shouldn't be jealous. The last thing he needed was to be trapped with her in close quarters for the long ride to the mainland, not while she was another man's woman. "Good. Guy likes her just fine."

"Guy can't spare two or three days." Seamus sighed. "If it's such a problem, tell her she can't go. Tell her I said to give you a list, and you'll take care of it."

That was cowardice. Defeated by a woman's disregard, or admitting himself the sort of monster who couldn't be trusted to keep his wants and needs to himself. Brooding about it had been more enjoyable before Seamus offered an out that made him feel like a boy. "I'll get it done. We're all doing what we have to, this winter, and I have to deal with my instincts."

Seamus nodded. "Then I trust you'll handle the situation as best you can."

Victor watched as the last of the wolves filed toward the door, trailed by Simone, arm in arm with curly-haired little Rose. Only Joan remained, but she seemed fixated on the jumble of papers spread out on the table in front of her, more of her damnable lists. Victor considered lowering his voice, but it would be pointless—anything Joan wanted to know, Seamus would tell her. "Nothing will help but time. For *both* of us. Her

134

instincts aren't settled yet either, but for all I know she doesn't know how."

The alpha shook his head. "Simone's been a wolf for long enough. Almost ten years."

"Instinct can be warped. You know that as well as anyone. She may not be damaged, but she's still..." *Hurt.* His wolf raged at the thought, but it didn't make it less the truth.

Seamus turned away from Joan and pitched his voice low enough to keep his words from his mate's ears. "Do you need to talk about it?"

"No. They'll realize they're safe here, and they'll get better."

"You're right." Seamus handed him an envelope. "You remember what time to meet Slim?"

"Don't be insulting." Victor tucked the envelope into his vest pocket and grinned. "Old bastard is making a fine living on keeping us off the radar."

"With the number of times his brother hid us from the police over the years, he deserves it."

"Can't argue with that. I was planning on leaving tomorrow, just in case I needed an extra day. Don't want to stay long after meeting up with Slim—I don't like cutting the full moon too close."

"Understood." Seamus clapped a hand on his back. "If I don't see you before you leave, have a safe trip."

"I will." Victor raised his voice. "You can stop pretending you're not listening, Joan."

Joan flipped over a page without looking up. "You're not nearly as enthralling as you think, Mr. Bowen. Your manly posturing was amusing for a time, but the pouting is less interesting."

Seamus choked on a laugh. "Not very subtle, love."

"He's not a subtle man."

Victor couldn't even muster up a reasonable level of outrage—Joan wasn't a woman whose company he enjoyed, but her pointed comments occasionally struck home. "No, I'm not a subtle man. I've been a werewolf all of my fifty-three years. In five decades, you won't be so damnably refined either."

Joan actually laughed, and it made him dislike her a little less. "You may be right. I feel at least ten percent less refined already. Seamus? Are you almost ready to leave?"

"In a moment." He shoved both hands in his pockets. "I'd like to tell Simone about the trip, Victor. If you don't mind."

Victor hadn't been looking forward to the task, but long familiarity with Seamus made him suspicious. "Don't fuck around in my affairs, Whelan. I don't need a nursemaid."

"And I don't fancy myself one."

"As long as we understand each other."

"Clear as crystal." Seamus beckoned to Joan. "Come on. We have a few more things to do."

Joan shuffled her lists into order and rose, then destroyed any tender feelings she might have engendered in him with a slashing look. "Don't play games with my friend and her heart. She deserves better than that." She didn't have to continue, because her unspoken words hung like ice between them. *Better than you.*

The barb struck its mark, as she must have known it would, but Victor refused to let her see just how much. "If you're worried about the state of your friend's heart, best check with the wizard she's given it to."

"Joan, stop." Seamus closed his hand around her elbow and drew her toward the door. "Victor is more of a danger to his own heart than Simone's."

Friend or not, *alpha* or not, Victor was going to punch

Seamus in the face for saying it out loud. Later. "You two tend to your own hearts and leave mine and everyone else's alone. We have better things to do on this damn island than matchmake. Things like survive."

Seamus ushered Joan through the door, then turned and faced Victor. "We *will* survive, but we also have to consider life beyond that. I don't want everyone on this island alive but miserable. Especially not my friends."

Victor would worry about life beyond survival when he knew survival was assured. "One miserable winter isn't going to kill anyone. Not even your friends."

"Suit yourself." Seamus ducked his head with a nod. "I'll see you in the morning. If not, when you return."

"Have a good night, Seamus."

His old friend followed Joan into the night, leaving Victor to make his way down the path toward the dock and the solitary row back to the privacy of his sailboat. The winter was cold already, even now when it had barely begun. A long, miserable winter indeed, and something told him the cold wouldn't just come from the outside.

If he'd been a different sort of bastard, he might have been willing to take advantage of the bevy of young women whose instincts drove them toward the stronger wolves. Plenty looked at him with hungry eyes, and he flattered himself that not all of that hunger was for safety and protection. A selfish man might pick one of those sweet, pretty girls and while away the winter in a less lonely bed.

Too bad the sharp edge of responsibility cut both ways. Any safety he could offer would be a lie. Taking one of the girls before she'd found her footing would be abusing the instincts he'd been born with, instincts their corrupt Boston alpha had brutalized until none of them knew the power that came with the gift of their trust.

They'd learn. Even if it meant Victor had to beat every last man on the island to give them the space to do it.

Every man except the one he longed to test his strength against. Victor's hands clenched, and he forced himself to relax them as he rose. He might like the idea of chasing the wizard around the island, but James wasn't using anything against Simone but his too-damn-pretty smile.

Simone felt pulled to Victor because his wolf could meet hers. Protect hers. No instincts drew her toward James. In fact instinct very likely demanded the opposite, proof enough that she cared for the man in all the human ways that mattered. Human ways Victor would respect, even if it killed him, day by day.

Maybe it wasn't too late. Maybe Victor could give her someone to connect to—show her a man instead of a wolf. Maybe he could try the radical fucking experiment of talking to her.

It was worth a try. If it didn't work, there'd be plenty of time for a slow death by honorable retreat.

Chapter Three

Simone had never noticed how small Victor's sloop really was. It looked huge compared to the boat Guy used to fish, but it seemed to shrink with each passing minute as they sailed toward Searsport.

Victor brushed by her again to adjust a length of sail here, or to secure a rope there. She tried to stay out of his way, but it seemed there was no such thing on a boat. Every time she moved to a new spot, that was where he needed to be.

Finally, she broke the uneasy silence. "Is there someplace where I can be less of an inconvenience?"

He hesitated, his gaze flicking to the cabin door, which remained closed. After a brief moment, he nodded to it. "If you're cold, you can go down below. I should have offered before. I'm sorry."

"I'm not cold." She'd worn extra layers in preparation for the trip, but so far the weather had been surprisingly pleasant. "What I am is in the way, as I'm sure you've noticed."

For once, Victor smiled, and it lit up his brown eyes. "A little, but not as much as you think. Not unless I'm bothering you."

"No." Certainly not enough to go below deck to his cabin. She already knew he slept there, and envisioning him between the sheets, waiting for— "I'd like to stay up here."

"Fair enough." He eased past her, brushing her arm with his. "We've got another two hours of sailing, at least. Maybe we could come up with something to talk about."

Simone blinked. "You want to talk to me?"

He actually winced. "Christ, am I that much of an inadvertent bastard?"

"No," she insisted immediately, but she couldn't think of anything else to reassure him. Instead, she stared up at the clouds overhead and struggled for an inoffensive topic. "We could talk about the weather."

"We could. See anything interesting in the clouds? Dragons, monsters...pretty ladies?"

He was flirting with her. She couldn't stop the smile that curved her lips any more than she could stop her teasing response. "No. I do see a handsome but forbidding man, though."

"Well that rules out Guy. The man couldn't forbid water from running uphill."

"He does carry a certain ease about him," she agreed. It was an ease Victor lacked, but it hadn't kept her from being drawn to him. "Forbidding doesn't always mean bad things. The sea is as forbidding as it is beautiful."

"I love the sea." It sounded like an admission, quiet and a little self-conscious. "I grew up in the west. On the plains. The prairie goes on for miles."

"Really?" This tiny glimpse was more than he'd ever willingly shared before. "I traveled through once. On the train, going to California. With all that grass, it felt like being out in the middle of the Atlantic."

"Mmm." He did something with one of the ropes that inched the sail to the side, and the canvas snapped under the strong wind. "I was a cowboy for a while. Not the best job for a werewolf, but at least I healed fast."

The urge to close her eyes and imagine him roping calves, covered in dirt and sweat, was almost overwhelming. "Did you like it?"

"Wasn't quite as glamorous as the stories make it sound, but it was a job. My nephew still owns the ranch, though it's not much to see right now."

She wondered if the ranch was like the rest of the drought-plagued land she'd heard about, dust-dry and overworked and blowing away in the wind. Maybe it was whole, dead but still rooted together and waiting for rain. "Bad times come and go," she whispered. "They can't last forever."

"No, they can't." His voice held sorrow. Exhaustion. "Werewolves have long memories, though...and times are pretty bad."

What had happened to put that look in his eyes? What had driven him from his home, all the way to New England? Maybe he would share it, in time. For now, Simone felt as though the slightest push too hard could shatter the fragile truce they shared.

So instead of questioning him, she smiled gently. "You've been a cowboy and a bootlegger. What else have you been, Victor Bowen?"

"Farmer. Smuggler." He returned her smile, a hint of mischief sparking in his eyes. "Gambler. That was fun. More fun than lobster fisherman."

He had a beautiful smile, one that shocked the truth out of her. "I've never been anything."

Both of his eyebrows crawled toward his forehead in an expression of polite disbelief. "You and Joan have done quite a bit."

"Joan has." She hadn't meant to sound so lost. Ashamed. "I

just follow along after her."

"That's what makes them alpha," Victor replied, tone firm. "She and Seamus both. Being strong or dominant or just stubborn, none of it matters compared to that spark. They want to lead. No shame in following someone like that."

"Perhaps you're right."

"No perhaps about it, doll. Guy may be easygoing, but he's a strong wolf. So am I, and a lot of the men who follow Seamus. Doesn't say anything bad about us, just good things about him."

What he couldn't know was that Simone had been the same way before meeting Joan. She'd allowed herself to be swept along, with no real control over her own life. "Right." She tilted her face to the sky and the clouds again. "There's one that looks like a ball gown."

He didn't try to change the subject back. "My brothers would have counted that as a pretty lady."

She couldn't resist a wink. "Because it curves in all the right places?"

"Like all the best things in life."

Sometimes, like now, he looked at her like he wanted her, after all. Like she belonged in his arms. "Too bad I'm not wearing a fancy dress. You could be my Prince Charming."

"A prince with a dubious past, maybe." He looked away from her, reluctantly enough to light a warm glow of hope inside her. "You don't need a beautiful dress. You make trousers and paint spatters elegant."

I want you to kiss me. An ill-advised plea, because it would only renew the uneasy tension between them. "Thank you."

A gust of wind snapped the sail again, filling the suddenly awkward silence. Victor studied the horizon, then cleared his throat. "I think we might have a squall headed this way. Might be best for you to go below and stay out of the rain."

Before she could argue, a fat drop of rain splashed on her cheek, followed by another. Simone laughed and rose. "Consider me convinced. Yell if you need me."

The area below deck was small, just shy of cramped. A sleeping berth occupied much of the available space, its width smooth and neatly made up. She sat on the edge of the bunk, unable to resist the urge to run her fingertips over the coarse blanket.

It was warm, but too rough. Victor needed a quilt, something heavy enough to hold off the chill but more comfortable than the loosely woven wool. The blanket would make decent batting, though, and perhaps she could talk him into letting her sew something—

A dangerous train of thought, far more so than her earlier imaginings of him naked in this very bed. One was about sex, pleasure, and the other...

Intimacy. The small cabin heated quickly, and Simone peeled off her coat. A wooden crate wedged beside the bunk held books, and she lifted them one by one, curiously examining the titles.

The crate held everything from travel journals to several works of Shakespeare. A crisp ten-dollar bill had been placed in a battered copy of *Macbeth*, and she opened the book to the scene, late in the play, of soldiers marching on Dunsinane Castle.

Had he put the bill there for safekeeping, or did it mark his place? She laid the book back in the crate, and it brushed free a photograph which had been tucked behind a slat.

It featured a large group—a family, judging by the resemblance—bearing the careful smiles and stilted poses of a studio photograph. The father and mother were easily identifiable, and she counted thirteen children, with ages ranging so widely that some were no longer children at all.

Like Victor, who stood tall at the back of the group, looking only a few years younger than he did now. Simone studied his face, even drew her fingers across it before snatching her hand away.

These were Victor's personal things, his *private* things, and she had no right to be rifling through them. He'd offered her the hospitality of his cabin. She couldn't repay it by nosing around in his belongings.

Simone replaced everything and stretched out on the bed. The warmth of the cabin combined with the movement of the boat lulled her, but even more comforting was the way she could smell Victor on the blanket and pillow.

As she drifted off, she had to admit that his scent, more than anything else, was what soothed her into sleep.

They sailed into Searsport harbor under an overcast sky. Victor had a feeling that Simone had drifted to sleep, cocooned in the warmth of his bed, but that was an image so stirring he didn't dare give fantasy the weight of reality. It would be bad enough to return to sleeping there with her scent wrapped around him, a scent that wouldn't fade for days.

A part of him—and not a small part—warmed in anticipation.

Slim had come through with the first part of their deal, at least—securing a slip for him in the busy harbor. Victor docked without hassle, tying off with the help of a young, hungry-looking boy who probably expected a few pennies and went wide-eyed when Victor pressed two quarters into his small, dirty hand. The boy folded his fingers over the treasure before anyone else could catch a glimpse, and Victor hid the ache in his chest beneath a smile.

The boy shoved the coins into his pocket, murmured his thanks, and departed so fast the wooden dock trembled under his tiny worn shoes. Victor hopped back onto the boat and spent a few moments steadying himself with the boring minutiae of tying down sails and checking lines, using the comforting routine to find his balance.

Guilt intruded, just as it always did. All too easy to see a cousin or nephew in that young boy's place, hanging around docks or city street corners, desperate for any job that might put a few cents more in the family pocketbook. The last word from the family farm had been more desperation, more poverty.

He'd sent more money than the place was worth over the past few years. The first three times he'd had it returned, his proud, upstanding family unwilling to accept money earned in a life of crime. Then the crops had failed in 1930, and the next letter he sent came back only with stiff gratitude. Proof of the depth of their desperation. Proof of *everyone's* desperation.

In his darkest moments, he could almost understand how so many of the werewolf packs had gone so bad, so fast. Maybe civilization among wolves had always been the dream, and this was what they were meant to be. Savage, desperate beasts, fighting over the scraps the weak were unable to protect.

Instinct revolted. He fisted both hands and dragged in a deep breath, tasting rain—or even snow—on the biting, salty air. Brooding could wait until he'd gotten Simone into town, hopefully ahead of the coming storm. With his head full of plans for finding an inn and making the most of their time on the mainland, Victor almost forgot what would be waiting for him when he eased open the door.

Simone was stretched out on his bed, looking sweet and comfortable, like she belonged there. Her scent had already twined with his, marking this place that had been his sole domain since he'd purchased the boat.

She groaned and rolled over, curling her body into a ball to ward off the chill of the air. "Not now, I'm sleeping," she murmured.

Victor slipped into the small cabin and pulled the door shut. "Sorry, darling, but it's time to get a move on. We're in Searsport."

Wide blue eyes blinked open, and Simone struggled to prop herself up on her elbows. "Damn, I slept the whole trip."

The movement arched her body, lifting her breasts, and inconvenient arousal stirred. How easy it would be to slide over her, to sink home into the cradle of her hips, feel her long legs wrapped around him. He could make her arch like that out of ecstasy, show her the pleasure to be had when a strong wolf set about claiming his mate.

His mate. Tripping over the words returned sense before he made the painful mistake of giving into need. She wasn't his mate. She wasn't *his* anything. Disappointment and confusion deepened his voice, made it rougher than he wanted. "Not a problem. But now we'd best get going."

Her eyes clouded with uncertainty, but she only nodded. "We have a lot to do."

He was doing it again, taking his frustration out on her. Victor dragged his temper under control and moderated his tone. "Yes we do. I'll wait up top."

Victor didn't wait for a response, just turned and fled, damning himself as a coward.

Simone flipped over the creased paper in her hand and marked off two more items on the list as she took careful inventory of the purchases remaining on the bed.

Most of the crates contained fabric, and she'd arranged for more bolts to be delivered to the dock the next morning. They could spend the winter making clothes and linens enough to supply them all.

One less thing to worry about. Still, she dropped her pen and rubbed at the knot that had formed between her shoulders. There were so many things she'd never considered being without until she'd had to make practical arrangements for just that. Come spring, they'd have time to dig more wells and build real houses, all with the appropriate amenities and fixtures. Until then, they had to make do.

It was exhausting.

The creak of a squeaky board outside her room warned her a moment before a soft knock sounded against the door. "Simone?"

She tensed, then told herself she was being a ninny. "Come in, Victor."

He stepped inside and closed the door gently behind him. "How was your afternoon?"

She wished—for the thousandth time—that looking at him didn't make her chest squeeze tight with longing. "Productive and expensive. Yours?"

"The same." He moved toward the bed, gaze fixed on the fruits of her shopping excursion. "What is all of this?"

"A little bit of everything. Fabric for clothes, some kitchen gadgets, incidentals. All very boring but necessary." She climbed off the bed and smoothed her skirt, cursing the vanity that had led her to dress nicely. He'd probably think she'd dolled herself up for him, and the hell of it was that he wouldn't be entirely wrong.

He brushed his fingers over a cream separator, his attention still fixed on the bed. "What's this?"

147

The last thing she wanted to talk about was the latest in dairy equipment. "It's for the goats' milk. It doesn't separate well, but we can use this to—" He looked up at her, and her breath caught.

Hunger. In the split second before he glanced away she saw it plainly in his eyes, along with a very male appreciation. He dropped the separator back to the bed and cleared his throat. "Would you like to find some dinner with me? It might be your last chance to go to a restaurant for a while."

Even sharp disappointment couldn't overcome practicality. "I ate a late lunch, but thank you for thinking of me."

"You sure? I clean up all right, for a farm boy."

"A tragic understatement, I'm sure." She straightened his collar, stupidly grateful for the chance to touch him. "I don't know if my poor little heart could take it."

The muscles in his shoulder tensed a moment before his hand shot up, curling around hers. Rough, warm fingertips brushed her skin, urging her heart into a staccato rhythm. "I'd be gentle with your heart."

"Would you?" Perhaps he'd been trying, though every short word and cross look had stung.

He closed his eyes, though his fingers kept up their slow, maddening stroking. "You gave it away before I had a chance to know how much of what you feel for me is instinct and how much is real. I'm not the kind of bastard who'll take what was never offered."

She blinked at him as she tried to process his words. "Are you talking about *James*?"

Victor tensed. "Who else would have a claim on you?"

No one—not even James. She jerked her hand away. "You're an ass if you think I'd look at you the way I do after giving myself to another man. An *ass*, Victor."

"Plenty of your girls look at me," he ground out, frustration vibrating in his voice. "They look at the other strong men too. They can't help themselves. No one has taken care of any of you the way they should, and your instincts are starving."

Her hand itched to strike him, and her eyes burned. "Believe what you want. *Do* what you want, but don't say I never offered you anything, because it just isn't true."

Victor surged forward and caught her shoulders. "Tell me it's not true, that you're not fighting your instincts."

If only it were that simple, and her attraction to him was solely instinctive. "Of course I'm fighting them. I don't want to pant after a man who runs in the other direction when he sees me. It's humiliating."

He bit off a curse, and in the next heartbeat his mouth crushed against hers, hard and open and so very hot.

She should have pulled away. She should have *slapped* him, especially after he'd all but accused her of not knowing what the hell she really wanted. Instead, she clung to him as pleasure mounted.

More pleasure than should have been possible from a single kiss, except that he tasted like heaven and felt even better. Simone touched her tongue to his and moaned helplessly.

A lifetime later he lifted his head with a groan, both hands sliding up into her hair, cupping the back of her head. "I shouldn't do this. I shouldn't—" He bit off a curse, and his fingers tightened. "I want you beyond reason," he whispered and claimed her mouth again. Slower this time, his tongue teasing apart her lips as he tilted her head back.

Simone leaned against him, her head swimming. This was what she'd always glimpsed in the moments before he turned away from her, and she wanted more. So much more.

Her fingers tangled in the front of his shirt, fumbling with the buttons. "Victor."

He caught her hands and took a tiny step back. "No, too fast. Dammit, Simone, you may think it's foolish, but it's the way I was raised. You've been through hell these past few years. A good alpha protects."

He was doing it again, making assumptions about her state of mind. "Some of the women on the island have had a hard time, but *I'm* fine. Please stop presuming to know how I feel and why."

Doubt clouded his eyes. "You didn't say you hadn't had a hard time."

"Haven't *you* had a hard time? Hasn't everyone? I don't know what you want me to say." His hesitation was insidious because it stemmed from such genuine concern that she almost forgot how dangerous it was. It would be too easy to tell herself that he only had her best interests in mind—and let him walk all over her.

She took a deep breath. "It's one thing to protect, or to want to take things slow, but it's another not to trust me to know my own feelings."

"And the wizard? Does he know your feelings?"

"Yes. Unlike some people, he's bothered to ask." Lingering guilt sharpened her tongue. "Why do you persist in bringing James into every conversation? This has nothing to do with him."

Victor's expression of disbelief might have been comical, under other circumstances. "You spend your time with him. You share meals with him. The whole pack thinks you're a couple, and you haven't been quick to dissuade them."

Because it hadn't mattered, not with Victor doing his best to avoid her. "I enjoy spending time with James. I wish I enjoyed it more," she admitted, sick with misery. "All he wants is to love me, and I hate that I can't give him that."

"Simone, this isn't—" He closed his eyes and rubbed one hand over his face and stubbled jaw. "You may know your mind and heart, but if you would play games with your instincts, then you don't understand them at all."

She crossed her arms and rubbed them to ward off the chill that shook her. "I'm sure you're right." She didn't understand anything, least of all why instinct would lead her to torture herself by seeking Victor's reluctant attentions. "Can you see yourself out, please?"

He backed toward the door, then turned with his fingers curled around the knob. "This isn't a game to me. I was born a wolf, and I don't know how to play. Not about this. A woman is a warm body, or she's everything. You're more than a warm body, but if even part of you wishes you loved a wizard, you're not ready to be everything."

It was too much to bear. He'd done nothing but push her away, and now he was blaming her, *punishing* her, because she'd allowed herself the comfort of a friendly face. "How could I be ready to be anything to you when you act like you hate me?" she whispered.

His voice dropped. Gentled. The infuriating tone of a man trying to manage an irrational woman. "I don't hate you. You know I don't hate you."

It would be so easy to give in and rage at him, but it would only cement his conviction that he was right. "How am I to know that, exactly? From the way you glower at me? Perhaps your strict policy of avoidance at all costs."

"I don't—" His jaw tightened, and his irritation evidenced itself in a dark wave of power with guilt riding hard on its heels. "It wouldn't be fair to you."

"I'm not asking you to fuck me, Victor." Her own hurt and

151

anger lent her voice a steely edge. "I'm asking how I was supposed to know your mind on any of this."

He winced at the blunt language. "I wasn't referring to sex. It's not fair for me to be around you when I can't control myself. I'll influence you without meaning to."

"I'm not weak-willed or feeble-minded. I can make my own decisions!"

A growl filled the room. Victor stalked across the intervening space, and magic came with him. Wild and oppressive, the sense of *him* filled the room. Strong. Dominant. He stopped a few inches from her and growled one command. "Sit."

She didn't *want* to. She wanted to face him, to stand strong and tell him that she was her own woman, no matter what alpha control games he wanted to play.

Stand, Simone. Don't *give in.* But her body moved anyway, and she couldn't choke back an angry sob as she dropped to the bed.

He stumbled back a step, then swore. Power vanished so fast she thought her ears might pop. "God *damn* it, Simone, I shouldn't have—I didn't mean..."

Looking at him hurt, so she dropped her gaze to the floor. "You've made your point."

Fingers touched her shoulder, tentative, as if he feared being slapped away. "It's a point I shouldn't have made. I'm truly sorry."

"No, you were right." She swallowed miserable tears. "I thought I could trust you."

An anguished noise escaped him, and his touch vanished. "You should be able to trust me. But when I'm around you, I don't trust myself."

"That's all you had to say." Simone wiped her eyes and

looked up at him. "I haven't been trying to torment you. I just..." *I wanted you so, so much.*

"I know." He reached for her again, his fingers soft at her jaw. "You're not responsible for making me control myself. You're not responsible for my actions, and you shouldn't have to worry about being safe with me. My failure, Simone. My fault."

No matter whose fault it was, they had both lost. "You should go. We have an early day tomorrow."

Regret filled his voice as he backed away. "If you need anything...I'm just next door."

"I won't." His obvious guilt drove her to speak, and she stood and squared her shoulders. "This has only proven that we—we can't be reasonable about one another, Victor. I won't be coming to you for the things I need. I *can't*."

He looked like he wanted to fight, but something held him back. "If you feel you can't, then I've truly let you down. Perhaps, some day, I'll prove myself again."

Except that she might be leaving come spring. "What if it's too late by then?"

A sad, lonely smile curved his lips. "Then I'll hope you don't hate me too much while you're living the happy life you deserve."

She couldn't hate him, even if he broke her heart. "Good night."

He didn't move. His hand came up, then froze, as if he didn't dare touch her. So she took his hand and guided it to her cheek.

"Simone." Her name was a whisper, twisted with longing.

"I'll be all right." The only thing she could give him, a desperate reassurance.

"I know." He stroked her cheek, his callused thumb rough.

153

"Believe me, I know. You're strong. You've been through so much, and you're still strong. Someone just needs to keep you safe until you realize it. Not just want it to be true. Until you believe it's true."

Even through the pain and the doubt, her body responded to his touch. "I don't feel strong."

"You should, darling. You stand right back up, even when an alpha snarls in your face and knocks you down."

"I suppose." Though she wouldn't have to if she could just *stand* in the first place.

He tilted her head back. "Tell me one thing."

There was so much she wanted to say, and so little that he would—or could—hear. "What is it?"

"Will you give me another chance to prove you're safe with me?"

"I don't question that. I trust you with my life."

For a long time he stared at her, his dark eyes intense. His gaze traced her face until she felt sure he was memorizing her features. Then he smiled. "It's a start."

Simone choked back the pleas, the promises. "We can discuss it further when we get home."

His smile widened. He leaned in, his dark hair spilling over his forehead as he tilted her head back a little more, just enough to meet a soft kiss. "Good night, Simone."

When we get home. The words echoed in her head as he left, closing the door quietly behind him. They had been anything but a warning, and she was ashamed of herself. She owed him the truth, not something that sounded like a promise, even if it was a promise she desperately wanted to give.

When we get home.

When they got home, she had to tell him she might be leaving. That it might not *be* her home for long.

Chapter Four

Victor eyed the blood-red horizon and slanted a look at Slim, who stood next to him on the dock. "What's that they say about a red sky in the morning?"

He scratched the side of his wrinkled face and squinted up at Victor. "Keep your ass off the water, that's what they say."

If only it were that easy. The pack needed the supplies. It was the only reason he'd risked the trip in the first place, especially this close to the full moon, but coordinating the delivery of the supplies with their own travel needs and Slim's schedule had already proven a logistical nightmare. He needed to be as flexible as possible.

He also needed to get himself and Simone back to the safety of the island instead of trying to find a safe place to change and run. After his lapse in control, he wouldn't blame her for dreading the prospect of spending the most primal days of the month trapped with a man she shouldn't trust. "It's a short sail, and I'm reasonably skilled."

"Don't have to convince me, skip." Slim shrugged and hefted another crate. "I'll be at home by a cozy fire. Talk to your first mate."

Victor's gaze slid to the cabin, where he could hear the faint sounds of Simone rearranging supplies. No safely tucking her below decks and out of his way on the return voyage—they'd survive a drenching in a cold winter storm, but some of the supplies might not. "She's a tough girl. We'll get through."

"Don't doubt it." He settled the crate on the deck, where one of them could stow it below. "That's the last of it. Tell Seamus and his pretty little wife I asked after them, will you?"

Victor choked on a laugh at the thought of prim little Joan consorting with someone so obviously connected to the shady side of life. Then again, the woman did sleep with Seamus every night. "Sure. I'll even leave off the pretty, just for you. Our alpha is mighty possessive of his new mate. Take care, Slim."

"You too."

Simone emerged from below, just far enough to toss a wave at Slim. "Stay warm."

He laughed. "Follow your own advice, sweetheart. You need it more than I do."

Victor hopped onto the boat and waited for Slim to toss him the lines. Maneuvering the small boat out of the slip was easy enough, and the sun balanced on the horizon as he navigated the busy harbor, mostly full of fishermen getting out onto the water. Concentrating on that gave him an excuse to ignore the effect Simone's close proximity was having on his self-control.

She was quieter this morning, almost subdued as she sat, gazing out over the bay. "Will we run into a storm?"

"Maybe. We're not quite sailing into the wind, but we probably won't make the island much before the weather rolls in. If it gets bad, you can squeeze down into the cabin, even if it's a little uncomfortable."

"I'm sure I'll be fine." She smiled a little, a world of sadness in the expression. "I won't melt, and I won't break down and weep if the wind musses my hair."

The thought was absurd. "Doesn't mean you should want to be miserable if you don't have to be."

"You're right, of course." She fell silent again.

He'd said the wrong thing. Again. "I don't think you're fragile. Just don't see the point in both of us being uncomfortable."

Simone didn't answer, not at first. When she did, her words had nothing to do with the impending bad weather. "I wish you'd told me. *Talked* to me."

There hadn't been time, though the excuse was weak. He wouldn't have done so even if they'd been trapped together with all the time in the world. *Which we might as well be now.*

He had to say something, so he cleared his throat and adjusted his grip on the tiller. "I've never been much good at talking. Not when it matters."

"What was wrong with the truth?" She turned to face him, something lost and hopeless in her eyes. "I would have waited, for as long as you needed me to."

An impossible tangle with no end. She had become friendly with the wizard because she'd assumed he didn't care. He'd guarded his feelings because he'd assumed she was already taken. But the way she spoke... "I'm telling you the truth now. Are you already promised to him?"

"No, not like you think. But...he's going to Europe in the spring, to help settle things between the wolves and wizards. And he... He—"

Ice flooded his veins. "You're going with him."

"Astrid's father—you never met Astrid. She died when we—" She twisted her hands together. "It doesn't matter. Her father has asked me to come with James. To help."

"I see."

Simone stared at him, her eyes wide and pleading. "It's *peace*, Victor. If I can help make that happen..."

He wanted to tell her that the wizards and wolves had been

fighting for generations and would battle for more to come. That it was hopeless. That breaking her own heart against the wall of other people's hatred would accomplish nothing.

Selfish arguments, when he couldn't promise her heart any more tenderness. "That is a great responsibility. A great...honor."

"Yes, it is." She bit her lip. "I'm not sure when I'll be back. I would try, though, if I had a reason."

As if he could compete with dreams of saving the world, however far-fetched. "You need to go where your heart leads you, Simone."

"Sound advice," she whispered. "Thank you for understanding." Once more, she turned away, putting her face to the wind.

Her pain trembled through him, even if she was too proud to show it, and it hurt. "I'm sorry."

"Don't."

"Do you want me to tell you to stay?"

"No." She breathed the word, her voice hoarse and weary. "You can't give me what I want."

The more they talked, the more twisted it became. Action suited him better, but the wind had already picked up, sharp with the scent of rain. He had to stay alert to keep them both safe. "If you followed your heart and it led you to me, I'd do my damnedest to make you happy. That's all I have to offer, and maybe it's not enough."

"I don't know *what* to do anymore," she confessed.

So tired. So hurt. Victor held out an arm without thinking and left it there, knowing she'd likely reject him. He still had to offer. "Come sit down."

She came, sliding to sit beside him. "Can we not talk about it? Not right now, at least."

"Of course." He slid his arm around her and tucked her close against his side. Comfort instead of romance, the casual touches of a pack, even if the feel of her pressed against him excited him. "What should we talk about?"

"The weather?" She laughed a little. "Perhaps I shouldn't have insisted we go back today."

"Even if you hadn't, I would have. Neither of us wanted to spend the full moon in Searsport." Though with the bite of the wind taking on a mean edge, they might soon wish they'd risked it, no matter their personal trouble. "This will only be our second full moon together as a pack. The girls need you."

"Yes, I suppose they do."

Maybe she thought he was trying to remind her how much she was needed now that he knew she might leave. "It'll grow easier in time. Once they become accustomed to the men."

"You sound like Joan." Simone tilted her head up and studied his face. "Why do you dislike her?"

Dangerous ground indeed. "It's not...dislike." Not quite a lie. "I'm wary of what Joan is, not who she is."

"And what is she?"

"So alpha it makes my head hurt."

"So is Seamus." She shrugged under his arm. "Why should that bother you?"

"It's a man's duty to protect his family. His pack. It's a responsibility but, in the end, we're expendable. Female wolves are precious. You shouldn't have to fight. Not saying Joan had a choice—but maybe now I wonder if she'll know how to stop."

Simone's brows drew together, and her back stiffened. "We're precious because we have babies and that's that?"

"You're vital because you have babies," he retorted. "You're precious because you're the reason life's worth living."

"I—" She stopped and sighed. "I can't even be irritated with your attitude when you say things like that."

Victor hid a smile. "I was born a wolf. Raised this way by a mother who would have thrashed me within an inch of my life if I implied her only worth was having babies."

Simone laughed. "I think I would like your mother."

His mother would probably like Simone too. "Maybe you'll meet her some day. She's liable to start talking to me again, now that I've given up my life of crime."

She touched his hand where it curled around her arm. "You're estranged?"

Another topic best left alone, though he found himself answering. "For the last decade or so. Maybe a little longer. So bad they'd barely accept money from me, even with the crops laying dead in the fields."

It took her a moment to speak. "It isn't pleasant, is it? Being cut off from everything you once knew."

"No, it's not." The wind was picking up now, blowing ominous clouds toward them. Snow or rain, either one would make for a miserable sail. Distracting her from it might be a blessing. "You speak like someone who knows."

"Yes." She snuggled closer, though she gave no outward sign of noticing the chill. "That's how I wound up with Edwin Lancaster. I was his mistress. His first."

Victor stiffened, his arm tightening before he could stop it. Edwin Lancaster had been a bastard—a selfish, self-absorbed ass of the highest degree. Money had given him the power to rise above his place in the pack, and he'd used that power to make women into wolves to serve as his playthings.

That Simone had been one of them shouldn't have been a surprise. Most of the women on the island owed the destruction of their lives to Edwin's womanizing. But Simone...

Protectiveness rose, and for a moment he regretted that Joan had killed the bastard. She'd probably let it happen too quickly. "I thought Joan was the first," he managed, mostly to have something to say. "Isn't that why he hated her?"

"No, Joan was the last. She defied Edwin, and she changed everything. *I* was the first." Her mouth twisted in a shaky smile. "I'm the one who let it happen, to myself and the rest of them."

That sad little smile couldn't hide her pain, and his wolf raged uselessly. There was no one left to challenge, no one to hurt for the discomfort she'd suffered. "You can't be held responsible for the ways you've been mistreated. The man was evil."

"You're excessively kind. The fact remains that I should have done something, if only for the other girls Edwin began to...collect."

"What could you have done? Fought him?"

"I don't know. *Something.*" Simone shivered. "Things worsened so gradually. He used to be different, you know. Not good or noble, but not as bad as he was in the end."

Most people didn't go bad overnight. He leaned down and dropped a soft kiss to the top of her head. "Times have changed many a man and wolf. And you went with Joan. She may have the will, but while she and Seamus were off fighting Lancaster, you were making those girls feel safe. That's what they need now, more than a warrior."

"Thank you." She stared up at him, her heart in her eyes.

If she'd looked dazed or worshipful, he could have resisted. If she'd looked young or lost or innocent—if she'd looked like *anything* other than a beautiful woman who saw something she wanted...

He saw heat. Respect. Desire. He saw that he needed to stop worrying about guarding her heart and start paying heed to his own.

Distant thunder rumbled as he lowered his lips and found hers open and ready. She kissed him eagerly, her fingers clenching in his vest, and murmured something against his mouth.

The tiller jumped under his hand, and he tightened his grip and willed the weather to hold. Just long enough for him to kiss her, to ease his tongue past her lips and taste the sweetness of her mouth. A groan rose inside him as he licked the tip of her tongue, demanding she respond.

Instead of letting him in, she pulled back and blinked away the rain that had splashed down and gathered on her lashes. "We bet against the weather and lost, I guess."

He'd never been so distracted by the taste of a woman that he'd failed to notice rain, and not a tiny drizzle. Fat drops landed on his head and slid down his neck, bringing an icy chill with them. Rain—for now. All too easy to imagine snow following if the temperature stayed cool. A sharp cold snap could ice the sails and rigging.

That was absolutely the worst-case scenario, but he still eased back from Simone. "You should see if you can tuck yourself down below. I'd feel easier with you out of the weather, and if it gets worse, I'll need to concentrate on getting us safely home."

She didn't argue, but she did pause before opening the cabin door. "If you need me..."

"Then you'll be wrestling with rigging in the freezing rain, whether you like it or not." He smiled at her. "Go, darling. I'll call for you."

She ducked below, then stuck her head back out. "Take care, Victor."

"I will." With her on the boat, he couldn't do anything less.

Chapter Five

After nearly an hour below deck, Simone's discomfort and fear had grown to epic proportions.

At first, she thought Victor might be able to pull them around the gathering storm. But the wind and waves mounted until even her limited and distant experience with sailing told her it couldn't be safe.

The boat pitched and rolled, and she had to press the back of her hand to her mouth and count to ten to quell her nausea. Her anxiety combined with her worry for Victor made her nervous, and she jumped every time a close crash of thunder shook the hull.

Water seeped under the cabin door, and she scrambled to block it. The door fit tight in its casement; how much water had to be dashing against it for any to make it inside?

Wind howled above her, and she pitched sideways, crashing into a crate as the boat lurched under her feet. A second later, Victor's voice rose from above deck. "Simone!"

She started to open the door, but it whipped out of her hand. Rain drenched her in seconds, and she blinked to clear her vision. "What can I do?"

Victor gestured her toward him with a wave of his hand. "Hold the tiller!"

He was shouting, and still barely audible over the pounding

rain and driving wind. The deck rolled sickeningly under her feet as he caught her hand and tugged until her fingers touched the smooth wood. He leaned close, putting his mouth next to her ear. "If we were both more experienced sailors, we could try to ride it out. But there are too many of these damn tiny islands and I'd rather pick which one we run into." He lifted his free hand and pointed straight ahead, where a dark line of trees was faintly visible through the rain. "It's big enough, if we can get there."

Lightning split the sky overhead, and Victor pulled away, leaving her to tussle with the tiller as he swooped down and snatched up something that looked like it had started life as a tin bucket. Holes had been drilled in the bottom, and a cord attached to the handle. It hit the water with a faint splash, and Victor let a few hundred feet of rope slide through his hands before securing the end. Then he set to work on the sails, his movements hard to follow with freezing rain driving into her face and dripping into her eyes.

The tiller jumped and jerked in her grip. Victor had angled the sailboat toward the wind and into the waves, but the closer they got to the shore, the choppier the ocean became. Water slopped over the sides and covered the deck, and she could only imagine the damage to the supplies below deck.

She wouldn't think what could happen if Victor lost his footing and went overboard. She'd have to abandon the boat, jump after him, and even then she'd be lucky to find him at all in the roiling water—

No.

The sickening swells gave way to rough, breaking waves, but they weren't quite as tall as they'd been a few minutes ago. The sea was calmer on the windward side of the island. A small sand cove beckoned, edged in wide sharp rocks but offering an oasis of relative calm.

Close. So close.

Victor paused in his work—just for a moment—and smiled at her through the rain. "We're going to be—"

A sharp gust of wind swallowed the words and tore the rope from his hands. The edge of a sail snapped out of his grip, and he swore and lunged just as the tiller lurched under her hand. She tensed instinctively, clutching it with all her strength.

Too much strength. Wood splintered as the handle snapped off in her hands. The boat heaved and rolled beneath her as it gave in to the demands of the wind, blowing away from the beckoning sand, straight toward the jagged rocks barely visible above the crashing waves.

"Simone!" Victor staggered, crashing into her as the deck tilted. He bore her to the wet wood, sheltering her under his body as he curled one hand around the side of the boat to hold them steady.

Even the wind couldn't drown out the sound of the hull being gutted.

It was over in three of her frantic heartbeats. The boat went eerily still beneath them, though waves still crashed against the side and washed over, icy brine mixing with the rain.

Victor lifted up, just enough to give her space to breathe. "We're not so far from shore. Can you swim?"

"I can make it." Her hair hung in her eyes, heavy and wet, and she dashed it away. "We'll help each other."

He shook his head and rose to his knees. "Once you're far enough away, I need to try to pull the boat free and get it beached. God knows how long we'll be here, and we may need the supplies to survive."

She wanted to argue, but he was right. Their survival could depend on salvaging the supplies, and that would be impossible if they lost the boat. "Be careful."

He dragged her to her feet, kissed her once, roughly, and stabbed a finger toward the water. "Go. I'll be right behind you."

Simone dove in, grateful she wasn't wearing a skirt that would tangle around her legs. It was difficult enough to navigate the cold water, even for a strong swimmer like her, and Victor would no doubt have a hard time wrestling with the crippled boat.

When she neared the shore, she turned to check on his progress. If he needed her help, then she'd give it, and he could yell at her later.

He'd tied no fewer than three lengths of rope to the front of the boat, and he swam with them crisscrossed around his body. He twisted and struggled with the load, and Simone almost started back in.

Before she could, he must have put feet on the rocky bottom, because he heaved toward the shore with a roar. Just like her swim, a human never would have been able to do it. Even with the strength of a werewolf, he fought and strained until the ropes had to have cut into his skin.

Finally, she trudged out to help him guide the boat, remaining carefully outside the snarl of ropes in case he slipped or the waves began to drag the boat back out to sea. Together, they hauled it onto the stony beach.

Simone stumbled back, panting. "What do we do now?"

He knelt and slid free of the ropes, his chest heaving. In answer, he gestured wordlessly toward a small boathouse down the shore.

It sat at the head of a short dock in bad repair, but the boathouse itself looked sound. The windows were intact, and a solid-looking door was securely latched on the side facing the shore.

Simone shoved her sopping hair from her face again. "Can

167

we fit ourselves *and* the supplies in there?"

"If there's a boathouse, there's probably an actual house too." Victor straightened too carefully, every movement slow and precise. "The tide's still on its way in. We need to get everything we might need off the boat."

He was hurt, but pointing that out would be useless. It would invite argument and accomplish nothing. He would never let her move all the supplies herself, much less go in search of a dwelling while she did. "Let's hurry."

They worked quickly in spite of Victor's injuries, and Simone took pains to reserve the most cumbersome crates and packages for herself. The first one earned her a sharp look and a grumble, but he was clearly too exhausted to argue. By the time they had unloaded half of their cargo, the howling rumble of the storm had grown loud enough to drown out conversation, and he *couldn't* complain.

Victor stashed the last bolt of fabric onto the top of the growing pile of packages in the sturdy little boathouse and nodded to the tiny space left, just large enough for a person to squeeze in out of the storm. "I'll see if I can find a house. It'd be a help if you could fill a crate with things we might be able to use. Food, blankets, whatever you think best."

"All right." Moving and possibly having to unpack and repack supplies would be more of a strain on him than searching the island, and she was glad to do it. "I'll listen out for you."

"Good." Lightning split the sky overhead, and thunder made the ground rumble beneath them as Victor leaned in and kissed her once, hard. "Stay safe."

Simone latched the door to keep it from banging open in the wind and began gathering supplies as best she could. She packed two crates, including a lighter one for Victor, and scrambled about to find his box, the one he'd already had

168

stowed in his cabin.

He'd left it behind.

She cursed and shoved open the door. It wasn't as though they couldn't save a picture and a few books, not if they were precious enough for him to keep in the first place.

The rain had worsened, and Simone dashed her hands across her eyes more than once to clear them. They'd left the cabin door open in their haste, and she splashed through ankle-deep water to retrieve Victor's personal effects.

Whatever lay in the bottom of the box was ruined, but some of it could still be saved. She hoisted it in her arms and shivered her way through the rain, back to the boathouse.

He emerged from the tree line, moving a little faster, as she reached the door. He waved an arm and called something, but the wind stole the words.

In a few seconds, she managed to consolidate the two packed crates and balance Victor's on top of it. Her muscles burned, but she didn't have far to go, and she kept even footing all the way up the small hill. "Did you find something?"

He reached for the small crate on top with a frown. "You shouldn't have risked going back for this. None of it will make life easier for us."

Only a few days before, his severe tone would have hurt her feelings. Now, she shot back, "This is important to you, and that makes it important to me. Besides, you can't replace it."

A noise escaped him, something between a snarl and a laugh. "You're irresistible when you're snapping at me."

Her cheeks heated. "You must be a glutton for punishment."

He just smiled and urged her along the narrow path as the wind whipped through the pine trees around them. "Up ahead. I broke in and lit a lantern—can you see the light from the window?"

She could see it, a small but steady glow through the gale. By the time they reached the cabin, she was drenched anew and trembling from the cold.

Simone dropped her burden on a dusty table, her teeth chattering. "Would a summer home like this have laid in a supply of firewood or coal?"

"There's some firewood here." Victor crossed to a wide, flat hearth and knelt. "I'm not sure how long it will last, though. I think we need to shift instead."

Simone studied the room for a moment—including the lone bed. "We can make a den, of sorts. If we draw that bench over and turn it on its side beside the bed, then mostly block the space under the foot there... With the two of us together, it should keep us warm."

Victor glanced over his shoulder to study the bed, then nodded and set aside the log he held. "If we lay out our clothes and blankets, they'll dry well enough on their own. We'll save the firewood for later, then, in case we need it."

"Good idea." She kept her silence as she unfolded several blankets.

The only problem with their plan was the fact that she'd have to strip out of her clothes in front of Victor. If the change had ever come easily to her, her nakedness would last a matter of moments. But she wasn't strong, never had been, and might end up grasping for that primal flicker of magic for long minutes.

With sufficient bedding spread out to dry, Simone bit her lip and hesitated with her fingers on the top button of her shirt. "How do you... I mean..."

His lips curved into a gentle smile as he turned his back on her. "I won't peek."

"Well, I figured you wouldn't—" The words hung in her throat as Victor's shirt slid from his shoulders to reveal dark, angry lines, a patchwork of bruises covering his back and sides.

She stepped closer without thinking, lifting her hand to hover over his battered skin. "Are you all right?"

"They'll be gone by tomorrow," he whispered. "But perhaps dragging a sailboat bodily to shore is a task even a werewolf shouldn't undertake."

"But you saved me." She touched him once and pulled her hand away. "Saved us both."

"And a few bruises are well worth keeping you safe, darling."

His voice had dropped to a low rasp. Simone knew she could touch him again, mold her palms to his flesh and shake his self-control. They could spend the day in bed, warming each other even under the scant covers.

Exactly what he'd told her he couldn't do.

She turned away. "Do you want to go first? I can hang your clothes and mine to dry."

"If you like." The soft slide of fabric followed, and the thump of his boots hitting the ground. Magic swelled, a dizzy rush of power that filled the cabin.

He'd accused her of being drawn to that strength out of necessity and instinct, like so many of the other women on the island. If it were true, perhaps she could have contented herself with a number of Seamus's other friends instead of wanting Victor so desperately.

The magic had the potential to make her feel safer, but it couldn't make her feel *needed*. It couldn't do what his hoarse voice and covetous stares did.

Simone swallowed hard and tugged the buttons on her shirt free, one after another, and spoke while she undressed.

"We can rest and warm up. Our clothes may not dry quickly but, if we get hungry, we can wrap up in the blankets that were already here and make something to eat. And then—"

Then, they could pass the rest of the day and the night curled together in the tiny den under the bed. It would be a torment all its own, not sexual in the strictest sense, but something even deeper—the trust that came with *pack*, mingled with the emotional attachment she'd already formed.

Emotional attachment. She shook her head as she gathered their clothes. It was just a harmless, pretty way to say she was falling in love with him, and there was nothing harmless about that.

By midday, rain had changed to sleet. Before dusk, it became a blizzard.

Victor ventured out as a wolf, braving the fat snowflakes coming down so hard they seemed to blow sideways, even through the sparse pines. He ran to the beach first, eying the wreckage of his sailboat with a sense of loss that seemed out of place in its depth. It was just a boat, after all, but it had been his home for the past month, his little scrap of privacy on an island bristling with too many wolves.

The rising tide had rushed through the gash in the hull and filled it with water. It lay mostly on its side, sail flapping in the stiff wind where one of the ropes had snapped. Even with supplies, it would take a skill he didn't possess to repair the damage.

Which meant they were well and truly stranded.

He circled wide on his way back to the cabin, scouting the area for signs of danger or intruders. The island was too small to hold a community, though he did find a second cabin. Rising on his back legs gave him a glimpse through the darkened window, but the building was even smaller than the one in which they'd taken up residence.

Still, the cabins meant that rescue *would* come, even if Seamus couldn't use magic or wits to find them before spring. Humans would return to check on their summer cottages. He and Simone simply had to make do until then.

He trotted back to the cabin and scratched at the door until Simone eased it open for him.

She closed the door quickly, clutching her blanket more tightly around her bare shoulders. "I found a kettle in that cupboard over there and started...something." She knelt by the hearth. "How's your boat?"

It was almost a relief to still be a wolf. He didn't have to answer the difficult question right away. Instead he walked to the far side of the room and did his best to shake off without getting anything important wet. Then he crouched low and started the painful process of shifting.

This close to the full moon, it wasn't easy. Embracing his wolf became effortless as the moon grew heavy in the sky, but reclaiming humanity turned into a battle. He rode out the pain as his bones realigned and fur vanished. Minutes later found him kneeling naked on the cold wooden floor, panting for breath as the fire lingered in his bruised body.

"All right?" she asked quietly, her gaze still focused on the contents of the iron kettle.

"I'll manage." Moving slowly, he wrapped up in the other blanket she'd laid out. It was dry, at least, through meager protection against the cold. "What are you cooking?"

"Soup?" A shy smile curved her lips. "If I sound uncertain, it's because I am."

The firelight cast intriguing shadows on her features,

turning her beauty into something haunting, and not touching her was a trial. "We'll learn to make do. I know a few things about rough cooking. No fancy kitchens where I grew up."

Finally, she turned her head and looked at him. "Rose has been teaching me to cook. I need a considerable amount of instruction, I admit."

"So that's why the two of you spend so much time together." He grinned to cover the way her voice stirred his body. "Perhaps she should be teaching all of us."

"You could attend her lessons, if you cared to learn."

"Maybe I will, once we get back to the island."

"You never answered my question." She tilted her head. "The boat?"

The answer probably showed in his eyes, but he shook his head anyway. "I think I'll be buying a new one in the spring."

She sighed and sat back. "We'll be fine here, but I worry about the others. Not knowing what happened to us, I mean."

There was nothing to be done about it, unless the wizard could work a spell to conjure them out of thin air—or, more likely, one to find them. "Maybe James will have a way of knowing."

"I had thought of it," she admitted, "but I don't believe he's acquainted with spells of the sort."

Of course not. The one useful thing the wizard could have provided, and he was incapable. Perhaps not a fair thought, but the man *was* a rival.

A rival with a distinct disadvantage. Victor had Simone to himself for the foreseeable future, after all. "Well, we'll do our best, and so will they. Seamus and Joan will take care of everyone."

"I know." She rose slowly. "What about you, stuck here with me? Do you think you'll make it?"

Her voice was light, teasing, but he couldn't summon an equal levity when she was so close. Days stretched out before him, just the two of them trapped in forced intimacy, and he *knew* his resolve would break. He could already feel it cracking.

"Now, that isn't fair," she murmured. "There should be a rule, you know. You aren't allowed to look at me like that if I'm not allowed to be encouraged by it."

He made himself look away. God only knew how much longer he'd have *that* much will power. "I think the rules are changing."

"So you've decided I'm not fragile and misled after all?"

Frustration rose as fast as desire had, a common enough occurrence around her. "I never thought you were either. I think you're reeling. I think we're all reeling. Or maybe you can't imagine the hell *my* instincts have been in with a dozen bruised girls looking at me like they might be considering fucking their way to safety."

"I'm sure I can, now that you mention it." She crossed the room to test some hanging clothes for lingering dampness.

"Is that so? What, exactly, do you imagine it's like?"

"I imagine you want to take what they're offering." Simone propped her hands on her hips. "Not because you want to fuck them, but because you know it will make them feel better, at least in the short run."

Close enough to be uncomfortable, though it fell far short of describing the true agony of being caught between the demands of his wolf and his conscience as a man. Instinct wanted to soothe the girls, to give them whatever they required to reassure them they were safe. Decency made him recoil at the idea of taking a traumatized young woman to his bed. And young they were, some of them sixteen or seventeen, too young for bedding, and far too young to be bartering with their bodies.

Given his choice, he'd bring Edwin Lancaster back from the dead and kill him again.

Victor dragged his temper under control with several steady breaths. "I think about what could make a sixteen-year-old girl ready to give herself to a stranger. I think about what pain, what neglect and abuse must have broken their spirits. I even think about the ones like Rose, who are older and quieter but flinch if you move too quickly, and I wonder how any of us can do right by you. How any damn thing we do won't be wrong somehow."

"So it's better to play games with us." Her eyes flashed. "Better to lie."

She was infuriating. "Lie? About *what*?"

"About the way you *felt*." She folded her arms around her body. "You lied every time you turned your back on me, and it hurt, Victor. Even if you had the best of intentions."

"When I turned my back on you, it wasn't a lie. And by the time it would have been one, I didn't need to turn my back. You'd turned yours. I was too late."

Instead of arguing, Simone bit her lip and sank to the bed, her shoulders sagging. "I'm sorry I brought it up. It doesn't matter anyway."

Defeat. She looked defeated, and it wiped away his frustration and anger, leaving behind the soft ache of failure. He had failed her, even if he hadn't meant to. "It matters to you."

"No." She breathed a soft noise of frustration. "You've explained your motivations, and it wouldn't be fair to expect more."

"Maybe not. But I never intended to hurt you."

When she looked up, it was with painful vulnerability. "*I* should have lied. Told you that you didn't have the power to hurt me."

Victor had to go to her.

He moved slowly, and her vulnerable expression gave way to wariness as she shook her head. "I don't need you to coddle me. It's silly."

She was wary, but she hadn't pulled back. "I'm hoping you'll coddle me a little bit, even if I don't deserve it."

After a moment, she unbent enough to favor him with a trembling smile. "You're doing this to humor me, I know you are."

"Then you don't know nearly so much as you think." He stopped just short of the bed and held out a hand. "I'm sorry, Simone."

Her humor faded, and she slowly laid her hand in his. "So am I."

She wanted him. It wasn't a new realization, but it was a thousand times more dangerous now that they were trapped alone, naked, with the moon singing in their blood. By tomorrow morning he'd be climbing the walls, horny and riled and in desperate need of a good run.

Or a good ride. How tempting it was to just give in and let instinct take the blame.

Tempting, and unacceptable. So he lifted her hand and kissed her knuckles. "Forgiven?"

Her gaze was soft and serious, and she answered in a wistful whisper. "Always."

Her sweet acceptance soothed the harsh edges inside him enough that he felt safe settling next to her and looping one arm around her shoulders. "We've both had a long day. Perhaps this isn't the time to be discussing serious issues."

"Or it's the very best time," she mused quietly. "We can't run away from anything."

"And we're too exhausted to be diplomatic?"

Simone laughed gently and leaned her head on his shoulder. "Sometimes I think trying to be diplomatic only gets us in trouble."

He loved the feel of her curled trustingly against him. "Trying to *talk* gets me in trouble. This is more than I've said in a month."

"That settles it." A pretty blush colored her cheeks. "We're truly opposites, in nearly every respect."

"Nothing wrong with that. I like listening to you talk." He brushed his thumb over her cheek. "We're going to be all right, darling."

"We're both smart and resourceful. Of course we will be."

"And they're going to be all right without us."

She barely hesitated. "If they can muddle through without the supplies, yes."

It wouldn't be easy, or they wouldn't have taken the risk of meeting Slim in uncertain weather to begin with. "Seamus has done more with less in the past, and Joan seems plenty stubborn. They'll make it."

"Then we only have to worry about ourselves." The back of her hand grazed his thigh through the blanket. "Tomorrow's the full moon."

That fast, he was rock-hard and aching with the need to touch her. "It is," he agreed, and even to his own ears his voice sounded hoarse.

"Things happen," Simone told him slowly, "and I need you to understand. To tell me it's all right. Because I wouldn't push you, Victor, not for anything, but tomorrow..." She swallowed hard.

The loss of control would be unforgivable—for him. But he couldn't put the responsibility for his actions on *her* shoulders. He cupped her cheek and kissed her forehead, ignoring the way her sweet, clean scent called to him. "Whatever happens, we'll manage. I'm not uninterested, it's simply not the way I would choose to be with you. It's less than you deserve."

"That isn't—" Her words melted into a growl, and she bit his jaw.

Jesus Christ. Her hair had dried in auburn tangles that knotted around his fingers as he fisted his hand in the disheveled mass. He dragged her mouth from his skin and nearly groaned at the sight of the smooth line of her throat, pale and vulnerable in the firelight. "It's less than we *both* deserve. Believe me, Simone, if you end up underneath me, I'll take you. I'll take you so completely you'll never forget the feel of my cock. And if you think I've been an asshole so far, you don't want to see me fighting to convince my wolf that you don't belong to me. This is not a game."

Her eyes fluttered shut, ginger lashes coming to rest on her cheeks. "So you keep reminding me. Do you think I would make light of something like this?"

"No. But last time I hurt you by not telling you why I pushed you away. Unless you've changed your mind about possibly leaving in the spring..."

She tensed under his hands and opened her eyes. "Making that decision now, based on this attraction, would be horribly selfish of me. Then again, so is this, isn't it?"

If it was, he was every bit as selfish. Arrogant ego whispered that he should stretch her out and show her just how good he could make it. Addict her to the pleasure of his touch, to the things he would do to her. With instinct riding her, they would wallow in animal need. He could almost taste her on his tongue already.

"Not selfish," he whispered, struggling to banish an image of firelight on her naked breasts as her hips lifted desperately toward his mouth. "Human. But it can't happen, not if we can help it."

She exhaled, one single shaky breath. "How big is this island?"

"I'm not sure." He loosened his fingers. "Large enough that there might be some game. Rabbits, at least. Maybe deer."

"Then we can go hunting tomorrow."

A different sort of chase. Safer, and necessary. "We can."

Her tremulous smile steadied. "Ready to try the vegetable soup?"

"Past ready. I'm hungry enough to eat Guy's cooking."

She affected a shudder and rose. "I figured you'd eat your shoes before going that far."

"They'd taste better." And he'd make jokes about eating his shoes all night if it kept that beautiful smile of hers alive. "Anything I can do to help?"

She waved him away. "You must have a hundred other things to do if we're going to be here for a while."

At least that many. Victor rose and stretched carefully, testing sore muscles. The hours spent resting as a wolf had accelerated his healing, which meant the bruises he'd earned getting them safely to shore would certainly be healed by morning. One look out the window, however, put to rest any ideas he'd had about braving the storm in search of more firewood. The wind battering the cabin walls showed no signs of abating and, even under the relative shelter of the trees, snow accumulated with impressive speed.

It would be a few days at least before Guy could risk taking his boat to the mainland. The island Victor and Simone had ended up on was just enough off the easiest course that rescuers from Breckenridge weren't likely to find them without magic. A trip to Searsport, then, and a phone call to Slim, who would have returned to Boston by now. Guy would realize they'd left the morning of the storm, and then...

Magic might be their only hope of being found before spring. At least their wizard would be highly motivated. Not the most pleasant thought, but Victor pushed down jealousy and possessiveness in favor of practicality—and protectiveness. It didn't matter who got the job done, as long as Simone was returned to safety. Whole. Happy.

His.

Victor's fingers tightened on the window frame until the wood creaked under his punishing grip. *Not* his. And somehow he'd find a way to remember that.

Chapter Six

The sun passed its zenith and began to sink in the west. Simone and Victor had spent the morning and afternoon of the second day trying to prepare the small cabin for a stay of indeterminate length, but they'd ended up snapping and fighting more often than not, even after their tentative truce.

It had to be the pull of the moon in her blood. It left her with immediate, unthinking reactions that were more animal than human, and her wolf wasn't comfortable with Victor's. They shared a bond, but it didn't hold the same ease she shared with the rest of the pack, all because they'd been too busy struggling not to give in to the greater intimacy they both desired. And uneasy wolves in their situation usually ended that wariness in one of two ways—sex or violence.

Fucking or fighting.

Victor hefted the rock he'd been using as a makeshift hammer and held out a hand. "Nail?"

She passed him one of the nails he'd pried from a chair. "Do you need another strip of wool?"

He stretched the fabric they'd salvaged from the wreck tight against the wall and nodded. "This is the least sheltered window."

And they couldn't spend all their time as wolves, especially her. When there was no moon, she could barely shift even if she *had* to. "How well-built is the other cabin?"

"It looked less sturdy than this one, but it did have a lean-to with firewood. Some of it might be drier than what we have here."

Worth checking, though maybe not tonight. It wasn't yet five, but the moon had already risen in the sky. If the gentle magic pulsing through her body felt like a flame, then Victor's must have been like a wildfire. "We'll have to stop soon."

"I know." He drove the nail through fabric, wood and wall with three swift blows, the hard muscles of his arm and shoulder straining against his shirt. "I can't hold on much longer."

Her first thought was to soothe him with her touch, but then she remembered that such a thing would only rile him further. "Do you mind if I get a head start?"

He shook his head, then thrust out a hand without looking at her. "Let me have the last few nails. I'll finish this up."

His control was clearly tenuous, and it made her feel better about running out on him. "I'll stay close," she promised, backing toward the door.

"No—" The rock hit the floor with a thump, his shoulders going tight. "Change in here. Please."

A growl escaped before she could stop it. "I don't think that's the best idea."

"You're vulnerable while you're trying to change. If you're not staying in here, I'm going out there."

She was more vulnerable near him, and if he hadn't figured that out... "Fine." Two buttons popped off her shirt as she tore it open, and she balled up the fabric and threw it at his head. "I'll do it right here."

The metallic sharpness of fresh blood filled the air. Victor opened his fist and the bent nails clattered to the floor. He drew in a deep, shuddering breath and let it out on a growl.

Then he moved.

His bleeding hand slapped against the door beside her head. Wild, heady power filled the cabin, more and more, until the walls seemed too flimsy to contain it. He lowered his mouth to hover over hers, stealing her breath and giving her his own. "You'll do it right here." A quiet whisper.

Another command.

This close, this *intense*, and still he held his body carefully away from hers. *Make me.* When she tried to say it, her tongue refused to move.

He smiled and licked the corner of her mouth, and she gasped as pleasure tingled through her. "So much fire in you, Simone. Even when you hold your tongue it burns in your eyes."

Sheer frustration drove her answer. "You don't know *how* hot I burn."

"Not nearly as hot as I could make you." The hand not against the door landed on her side, fingers warm against her skin. "Would you like that? If I slipped my fingers between your legs and showed you how to melt?"

Simone choked on a moan and scrambled to open her pants. "Touch me, Victor. Feel me."

He snarled and caught both of her hands, jerking them away from her body. For a moment she thought he intended to pull away, to leave her, but instead he guided her arms up, pressing her wrists against the door on either side of her head. "No going back," he whispered hoarsely. "Still want me to touch you?"

"Silly man." The truth was terrifying, and she gave it to him anyway. "Whether you take me or not, I'm yours. I belong to you."

All of the tension drained out of him in the space of a heartbeat. Victor pressed his forehead to hers and closed his eyes. "We'll change. Run. I don't want to be distracted trying to ignore the moon's call, because what I plan to do to you will take hours."

This close, she was loath to release him. "Kiss me, just once."

"Not just once." His lips curled into a smile before he pressed them to hers. Warm. Gentle, but unyielding.

Heaven.

Simone opened her mouth, straining toward him in absolute, utter need. Different this time, because she felt something new, something she'd only glimpsed in him before.

Possession.

He took his time kissing her, as if every moment before had been stolen and now he knew he could explore her at his leisure. His tongue swept along her lips, teasing one moment and strong the next, learning every inch of her.

She didn't realize she'd tried to move her hands until his fingers closed tight around her wrists. She bit his lower lip, a giddy sort of joy bubbling up inside her.

His chest vibrated against hers, a low growl she felt more than heard. He tugged away only to close his teeth on the edge of her jaw. "Accept me, sweetheart. Let me in, and I can help the change go easier. I have power to spare."

It burned inside him, a warm glow that drew other wolves like moths to a flame. "That isn't why. You know that, right?"

"Why what, honey? Why you want me?"

"Yes." She felt suddenly shy.

He smiled slowly, and it lit up his usually severe face. "I'm starting to believe that."

Her chest ached, this time with the words and promises she had to hold back. "Run with me. And tonight..."

"And tonight." He kissed her once more, then stepped back and closed his eyes. "Tell me when you're ready. I'll help you change."

Her pants hung open around her hips, and she pushed them to the floor with shaking hands. "I'm ready."

Soft power curled around her like a comforting blanket. It whispered to her wolf, coaxing her to life, and the readiness with which she responded surprised Simone. She barely had time to kneel before the spark of magic in her flamed and grew, bringing the change in a rush of heat and power.

In what seemed like moments, she stood on four legs, pawing impatiently at the floor. When he joined her, they could run, hunt.

Strong fingers stroked her head and the fur at the back of her neck, and Victor chuckled as he reached for the door. "Run. I'll catch you."

He didn't have to tell her again. Wherever she ran, he'd find her, sniff out her scent and chase her down. She almost lost her footing at the thought, then launched herself past the tree line and into the woods beyond the small clearing.

Almost immediately, gentle rustling and the scent of rabbit perked up her ears. She could stage a chase of her own, procure a gift for her future mate.

And then they'd hunt together, make this tiny island their own as the full moon strengthened in the darkening sky.

Victor ran them both hard.

Part of it was the need to explore the boundaries of their new home. The island was large enough to support animals and

186

a dense forest—good news for them in case they ended up having to stay until spring. The thick layer of snow on the ground made running a challenge, but it also made tracking fresh game laughably easy.

They hunted under the full moon until Simone's energy began to flag. She was a beautiful wolf, small and graceful and full of boundless enthusiasm. Satisfaction flooded him every time he looked at her, every time she came close and licked his chin or butted her nose against his jaw.

She was his, and she knew it.

Shifting back to his human form too soon would leave him feral and edgy, but staying a wolf too long would exhaust her. After a few hours, Victor began to herd her back in the direction of the cabin, willing to deal with his own discomfort to spare hers.

She caught on, but stopped short with a yip, and he had to nudge her on before she moved again. She paused again as soon as they cleared the trees by the cabin, watching him carefully.

He huffed and nipped at her flank, and she danced away and bounded to the door. He'd propped it open before shifting, so she had only to push it wide and run inside.

Magic rippled through the air as he ran in, and he found her already kneeling by the banked fire, her pale skin glinting in the dim light. "We'll have to stir this up."

Victor nudged the door shut and let her see to the fire. She had the advantage now. Freed from the call of the moon, she wouldn't fall victim to it again unless fear or pain brought the wolf to the surface.

He had a harder battle to fight. The moon hung heavy overhead and dug claws deep into his soul. The wolf struggled, demanding another chance to run and revel, to be free and wild.

Long minutes passed before he knelt trembling on the floor, sides heaving with rough pants.

"You didn't have to come back in," she murmured. "You could stay out. I'll be fine."

"So will I." *Eventually.* "I wanted to come with you."

The flames jumped and crackled as the fresh logs caught, and Simone stood slowly. "Can I help?"

She was naked. Beautiful. His to take. Even with pain lingering in his body, his cock stiffened. "That depends. Do you still want me?"

She tilted her head, and a coppery curl fell over her cheek. "I can't remember a time when I didn't want you."

The answer was everything he needed. He rocked to his feet and crossed the space between them, stopping a foot away to admire the wicked curves of her body. Full breasts, flared hips, soft, pale skin... "You're so beautiful."

She closed some of the distance, her fingertips skimming his arms as her gaze drifted down his body. "So are you."

He had to make it worth the wait. He had to make up for every moment of pain he'd caused her, erase it all and leave pleasure in its place. The bed was close enough to the fire to benefit from its warmth, so he swept her up into his arms and carried her to the rumpled blankets.

When he laid her on the bed, Simone bit her lip and held out her arms. "Seems silly to be nervous, but I am."

Victor had no idea if Simone had taken a lover after Edwin, and had no intention of bringing the bastard up now. Instead he slid onto the bed, into her arms, and kissed her softly. "Nothing to be nervous about, darling."

"It's easy for you." She wrapped her hands around him and pulled him closer. "Every time you kiss me, I turn to mush."

"Just because I'm getting harder instead of softer doesn't

mean you're not turning me to mush."

Some of the nervousness faded from her smile, and she teased one hand down his side. "An interesting point. One I'll have to bear in mind."

He would kiss her first, he decided. Kiss her until she'd forgotten what nerves were, then trace every inch of her with his tongue. She deserved a slow seduction. Worship. He'd claim her by pleasing her.

Her mouth opened under his, soft and needy, and she made quiet noises of pleasure. Before long, her body arched to his, hot and seeking.

The feel of her soft skin under his fingers drove him half-mad. He spread his fingers wide on her abdomen, sweeping his thumb up and down until she nipped at his chin, then gave in and swept his hand up to cup her breast.

Her gasp echoed in the quiet of the room as her nipple hardened under his palm. "Yes."

"You like this?" He teased his thumb over her nipple and delighted in the play of pleasure across her face. "Would you like my tongue? My teeth?"

Her breath caught, and she slipped her own hand to her other breast and echoed his movements. "Both."

So he gave her both, teasing licks giving way to soft nips as his fingers traced her hip and her waist and the soft curve of her belly—anywhere but the beckoning heat between her thighs.

As Simone's pleasure grew, so did her confidence. She smiled wickedly and rubbed her thigh against his erection. "Can I touch you?"

He couldn't deny her anything with that light filling her eyes. "Any damn place you want."

Her hand skimmed his stomach and his hip. "Here?"

If she wrapped her fingers around his dick, he'd explode. It might be worth it. "*Anywhere.*"

"Anywhere," she echoed softly, the back of her hand grazing his hard flesh. "It's been a long time, Victor."

An answer to the question he hadn't asked, and all the more reason to take things slowly. She'd tamed the feral edge of the wolf with her first hesitant smile, and it made it easy to roll onto his back. He tugged at her hand, pulling it up against his chest. "All the time in the world to get it right."

She sat up, kneeling over his thigh. "You won't hurt me."

The fact that it was almost a question made him want to hurt *someone*, but he refused to bring anger to bed with them, no matter its object. "Not in a thousand years."

Simone released a soft breath, one he doubted she knew she'd been holding, and bent over him until her lips met his bare shoulder.

It felt good—it felt fucking *fantastic*, but lying passively was its own sort of torture. He let himself thread his fingers loosely through her hair but didn't try to guide her. Instead he channeled the need trembling inside him into words. "I'm going to spend hours touching you. So many places I want to kiss."

"Here?" She kissed the center of his chest, then lower. "Or here?"

He tightened his fingers in her hair and lifted her head, giving her a deadly serious look. "I'll let you lick my cock like an ice cream cone if that's what you want, but you look me in the eye first and tell me *you* want to."

Again, that gentle smile. "I wouldn't if I didn't want to, but I do. I want to taste you."

Christ, he really *was* going to come like an overeager boy. And he didn't care, as long as she let him keep touching her. "Do I get to return the favor?"

She laughed and nibbled at his stomach. "Absolutely."

He was tempted—more than tempted—to drag her hips around and show her just what he could do with his tongue. Let her ride his mouth while she went down on him, see who lost it first. Tempting—but he didn't want any distractions when he made her come the first time. Not for him, and not for her.

Simone stroked his cock, lightly at first and then harder, her eyes locked with his. "I like the way you look at me."

"How am I looking at you?" It came out as a growl, but she didn't seem to mind.

"As if there's no doubt at all," she whispered. "Like you *want* me." She touched her tongue to the head of his cock, licking delicately.

No power in hell or on earth could have kept his hips from jerking up toward the heat of her mouth. "Like I'm imagining how good you'll look riding me?"

Her blue eyes darkened with passion. "Like you can't wait to sink into me."

"I can't." Victor drove his teeth into his lower lip to keep rougher words from tumbling out. He wanted to fuck her with his tongue until she was limp and trembling. Slide into her cunt before she finished coming. Watch her face when she realized she was *his*.

Her fingertips brushed his mouth, freeing his bitten lip, and she watched him closely. "Tell me what you'll do. What you want."

He caught her finger between his teeth with a low growl and teased at the tip of it with his tongue before releasing it. "I want to drag you up here and let you cling to the headboard while I taste you."

Simone froze, save for her deep, ragged breaths. "You want me on your mouth?"

It hadn't even occurred to him that no one might have bothered to see to her pleasure before, but she didn't seem nervous. "I want you everywhere," he replied, keeping his voice low. "But right now, I want you on my mouth."

She climbed higher on his body, her movements surprisingly graceful in spite of her haste. "You have to show me."

He caught her hips in his hands and held her there as she straddled his waist. "Depends on how you want to do it. Facing the headboard? Or stretched out on top of me with your head on my hip? You can touch me that way..." And the distraction would be worth it.

"My head on your *hip*?" She rocked against him.

Imagination conjured the feel of her lips around his cock, and he groaned. "Or do whatever the hell you want."

"That's what I want." She turned and stretched out over him, her nipples brushing his stomach.

The view of her ass, legs spread wide on either side of his chest, was almost too much. He smoothed one hand up the back of her thigh and dipped his fingers between her legs, groaning at the slick heat that greeted him. "It sure seems to be, darling."

She moaned and wrapped her hand around his cock again. "I don't know how many times I touched myself, thinking of you."

There was a thought to keep a man warm at night. "How do you like it? Slow and soft? Faster?"

"Slow, but not soft."

He gave her what she asked for, a slow, firm touch, letting the fitful movements of her hips guide him. She jerked and rocked, whispering his name, then lowered her mouth and slid her lips down around him.

Not even the need to make this the best damn sex of her life could keep him in control. He curled both hands around her thighs and guided her back until he could replace his fingers with his tongue.

Simone had been trying to get Victor in her bed for what seemed like forever, and now she wasn't sure what to do with him.

She enjoyed the taste of him on her tongue, musky and male and arousing as hell. It had to last, but she wasn't sure how long she'd be able to concentrate on teasing her tongue over his hard flesh, not with *his* tongue doing wicked things to her.

And wicked they were. He seemed determined to drive her crazy, taking his time exploring her and murmuring encouraging words, his hands never still.

She threw back her head with a moan, her whole body awash with dizzy pleasure. "Right—right there—"

Clever fingers pushed their advantage mercilessly, centering in on the spot that made her wild as his tongue licked and coaxed until she was shaking uncontrollably.

Bliss hovered just out of her reach, and she dug her nails into his hip. There was one thing she needed more than anything, so she pulled away and turned, positioning her hips over his. "Now?"

He caught her around the waist and flowed into a sitting position, fast and deadly graceful. His chest pressed against hers, his lips found her chin, and he moaned and coaxed her down, inch by inch, pushing into her. "*Now.*"

The seconds slipped by too quickly as he thrust up and she rocked down. Simone struggled to hold on to those moments, desperate to capture every second of his claiming. To burn it into her memory. "You're perfect."

"Only with you." He licked her shoulder and marked her with his teeth. "Because you're mine."

The need to hold his mouth to her skin left her clutching his head, tugging at his hair. "Again."

He curled his fingers in her hair and forced her chin up, ignoring her urgings in favor of licking a path up her throat. "Again, what? Tell me, darling. Let me hear it."

There was no room for shame or embarrassment. "Bite me again."

"Like this?" A soft nip as he dragged her down against him.

She couldn't speak, not right away, but she moaned her approval and scratched her nails down his back. "Harder."

He closed his teeth on her neck and growled. The possession inherent in the sharp caress sent her spiraling out of control, and she ground down against him.

"Just like that." He spoke the words against her skin, low and so hungry. "Perfect. We're perfect like this, when you're mine."

Perfect. Being with him was better than she'd hoped, an exact fit that made her want to weep because they'd wasted so much time already—

The thought evaporated like mist on a summer morning, swept away by the certainty that *this* was where she belonged. Where she needed to stay. "Always yours," she whispered.

His hands tightened on her hips, rough fingertips digging in as he urged her to move again, urged her to ride him, their sweat-slick bodies sliding against each other. The room filled with the sounds of their loving, skin on skin, and his rough, rasping pants and his voice saying over and over again, "I know."

Do you? She couldn't ask, could only moan as pleasure

closed tight around her.

Every rock pushed her higher, faster, until she couldn't have resisted if she'd wanted to. The sweet clench of orgasm seized her, primal and explosive, shaking her in his arms.

He came in the next moment, as if he'd been holding himself back by willpower alone. His guttural groan echoed off the cabin walls, the basest sound of satisfaction she'd ever heard.

It went on and on, an unceasing ecstasy intensified by the way Victor held her, as if he never wanted to let go. Simone gasped and shuddered as her tremors subsided into slow, easy waves of pleasure.

His fingers stroked down her spine. Soft. Worshipful. "You're perfect."

She felt full, complete. "Do you need to run again, or can you stay?"

"I can stay." He dropped his forehead to her shoulder, and she thought she felt him smile. "I feel downright tame."

"Tame enough to sleep?"

"As long as you sleep with me, darling."

"Nowhere else to go," she teased. "And nowhere else I'd rather be."

"Good." Both of his arms tightened, keeping her cradled against him as he fell back onto the tangled blankets. "That's all I need to know."

Sleep beckoned, and Simone snuggled closer. "Think we can keep each other warm tonight like this?"

His rumbling laughter made his chest vibrate beneath her. He shifted to the side and dragged at the blankets until they were both covered, and the edges tucked tight around them. "Sleep."

"Until I wake up, horny and groping you again?"

"Like I said, darling. You put those pretty little hands anywhere you damn well please."

"A waking dream."

"Uh-huh. Don't think you're so much waking as dreaming now, my gorgeous girl."

"Mmm." True enough, but he was warm and comfortable and everything about the world was... "Perfect."

Chapter Seven

By the time they made their way down to Victor's boat two days later, it was—in a very literal sense—utterly destroyed.

Simone picked up a jagged piece of broken wood and bit her lip, unsure of what to say. The boat had been his home, a private place on an island that had far too few of them. "I'm so sorry."

"It was a boat." His voice sounded tired. "I'll buy a new one."

She dropped the wood and turned to him. "It wasn't *just* a boat. It was yours. Part of you."

"So was my car," he retorted, and this time at least the words held a little bit of humor. "That's my baby Slim's driving around in now. We have things. We lose them. You don't live this long without learning things never matter."

"Not like people matter," she agreed, smoothing her hand over his collar. "You're safe, and that's what's important."

"We're safe." He leaned down and kissed her forehead. "I'll just buy an even nicer boat to make myself feel better."

"What do we do with this one? Anything?"

"Salvage what we can. The sails. Maybe the lumber." He picked up the piece of wood she'd dropped. "Too bad we didn't have an ax on board. Chopping down trees is going to be a challenge, if we need more firewood."

They could check over the other cabin, see if there happened to be even a handsaw. They could always cut up trees that had already fallen. "We'll figure it out."

"Without a doubt. Though if we could turn our minds toward some way of attracting attention to this island, it couldn't hurt. Guy will be out looking with his eyes, even if magic won't do the trick."

She should have been eager to find ways to hasten their rescue, but what had happened between them was so new it felt like one more misunderstanding, one wrong move could bring it to an end, and it left her wistful, wishing for more time.

Simone shook herself. "How familiar is Guy with these islands? If he comes out looking, will the smoke from the chimney catch his attention as something odd?"

Victor's shoulders bunched up in a half-hearted shrug. "Can't say for sure. I'm not willing to waste wood making more smoke, though. Not when we don't know how much of the winter we'll be spending here."

"Could we use part of the sail as a signal? Fly it from a tree out at the edge of the cove?"

"Maybe." Another shrug, this one accompanied by a smile that seemed almost a little conspiratorial. "We'll spend a few days thinking about it, hmm?"

Relief made it easy to wind her arm around his and smile up at him. "A few days, at least. I'm sure we can formulate a brilliant plan."

"With your brains and my appreciation of your brains? Absolutely."

"I do my best thinking in bed."

His lips twitched. "And here we finally got out of it for a little while. Miss it already?"

"How could I not?" Something about lying in his arms made

it easy to forget everything else.

Victor tossed the wood toward the water line, turning his back on her. His shoulders were broad. Stiff. "We need to talk. Or we need to decide not to talk."

It was far from unexpected, and Simone steeled herself for the discussion. "All right. Which would you prefer?"

He stared out at the ocean for a long time before looking at her. "Never was much good at talking, and seems like we've got enough to worry about for now."

She nodded slowly. "We don't know how long we might be here." Hurt feelings could only complicate that.

Something in his stance relaxed, and his easy smile returned. "I think the first thing we need to do is move the supplies up to the cabin. We may have to rearrange things, but having them on hand and in a sturdier shelter will be good."

It wouldn't take them long in fair weather and good fitness. "Can you show me the other cabin after that? I'd like to look around."

"Sure thing. Once we're situated, I think I'll go hunting. See if I can't find something for the stew pot."

"More rabbit would be helpful." She had no idea how long anything larger would keep with daytime temperatures hovering well above freezing.

He swept her a jaunty bow and affected a too-thick drawl. "I reckon I can rustle up a pair of bunnies for my lady's pleasure."

She couldn't help but laugh as she reached for him again. "You're insane, and I have to kiss you now."

"That was the point, darling." Then he kissed her, long and hard enough to make it clear that moving the supplies could wait.

Victor had lost track of the days.

He thought it had been six days since the full moon. Maybe a week since they'd crashed, except he couldn't be sure because he'd honestly forgotten to count.

Or maybe he didn't want to count. Sometimes, at night, with Simone curled against his side and her steady breathing lulling him towards sleep, he worried. About Seamus, trapped on an island with already traumatized wolves who would be frantic about Simone's disappearance. He worried about Guy, trying to decide between hauling traps and rescue missions, and sweet little Rose, who rarely seemed to talk to anyone but Simone.

Hell, he even worried about Joan, prickly Joan who must be sick with concern over her best friend.

Mostly, he worried that not even guilt could make him worry the rest of the time.

Day and night blurred together. He and Simone hunted and cooked and plotted increasingly outrageous and unlikely ways to draw searchers' attentions to their island. He made love to her in front of a roaring fire and spent hours trying to burn the pleasure of his touch into her skin. If he was enough...

No. Thinking wouldn't do him any more good than talking had ever done them both. He couldn't give her the words she needed. They twisted in his mouth and came out wrong, made her frustrated and angry. Instead he'd give her actions, he'd *show* her what he was. What he wanted to be.

He almost hoped rescue waited long enough for him to prove he would love her.

Next to him, Simone stirred. Victor rolled onto his side and drew her back against his chest, savoring the soft brush of her skin against his. "You awake?"

She chuckled low in her throat. "Not yet, but that could change."

"Too early." He loved the way her hip fit under the curve of his hand. "I was just thinking."

She lifted her arm, fingers brushing his cheek. "About what, darling?"

"Maybe it's just because I'm old, but living this way... It's not so bad."

Simone rolled to her stomach and propped up on both elbows, her tangled hair falling over her brow. "Living the rustic lifestyle, or the fact that it's just the two of us?"

His fingers itched to touch her hair, to smooth it into place—or muss it further. "The company certainly helps, but yes. I expected to miss the city more. Cars and electricity and telephones and the radio. I thought Seamus and Guy were mad when they proposed we hide on an island."

She smiled. "Those trappings of civilization turned out to be pretty empty, did they?"

"I wanted them all when I was young and poor and they were new and exciting." He gave in and brushed her hair back. "Now I just want a quiet life. A woman. Peace."

Simone's smile gentled, and she kissed his shoulder. "I think that sounds lovely."

So stay with me. Words he didn't dare speak. "Did you imagine you'd grow up and move to a near-deserted island in the Penobscot Bay?"

"Never." She laid her cheek on his chest. "I always imagined I'd grow up to be my mother. Marry a rich industrialist who was mostly content to leave me to my life while he led his own, and have several children I could mostly ignore, unless they happened to be making my life difficult."

As strong as his wolf had taken to her, he barely knew the

first thing about her. "I guess I knew you'd grown up rich. Didn't think much about it. You're not as..." he searched for a polite word and settled for a less offensive one, "...prickly as Joan."

"Perhaps it's because I'm older," she suggested, lifting her head. "Or because I dislike you far less."

"Good to know." He coaxed her cheek back to his chest and let himself stroke her hair. "How old were you when you became a wolf?"

"I had just turned twenty-one." She laughed again, almost solemnly this time. "A very misguided twenty-one, easily seduced by pretty words of devotion, regardless of their veracity."

Fucking Edwin Lancaster. "He must have had his share of pretty words. None of them should have been pretty enough to keep his alpha from kicking him into place."

"If it had just been Edwin, it never would have happened. He wasn't my first lover, Victor. Far from it." Simone sighed and sat up. "My parents sent me to college because they couldn't marry me off, not with my reputation, and they'd grown tired of trying. They figured I would graduate and go on to marry some rich but low-born man who needed the legitimacy of the Cabot name but couldn't afford to be too choosy."

Edwin would have fit the bill, since the Lancaster fortune was only a generation old. "So you found Edwin?"

"My parents did, yes. And by the time any of us figured out he didn't plan to marry me at all..." She shrugged. "It was easier for them to wash their hands of me. And I—" For the first time during her explanation, she looked uncomfortable. "I didn't have anywhere else to go. So I stayed and became his mistress."

"I'm sorry." Inadequate words, but the best he had to offer. "It shouldn't have happened the way it did. Once you were a wolf, the alpha should have protected you. You should have had a place to go."

She shook her head. "It's in the past. It brought me here, and that's the only reason it even matters anymore."

It would always matter to him. The pack he'd grown up in had been small—a ranch and a farm and the workers and kin who made their living on both—but the rules had been beaten into him as a boy by his uncle. Dominants protected. It didn't matter who the weaker wolf was, or who they should belong to. Humans ruled the world with their rage and fear, and wolves needed to help each other survive.

Like you're doing now. Breckenridge Island was a dream, the dream of safety. Sanctuary. "Nothing like that will happen to you again."

Her gaze softened even as it heated, and she stroked her hand over his cheek. "I know that."

Nothing soothed him like her trust. Not even her touch, sweet though it was. "Good. Just like I've been saying all along, darling. You're safe."

"I feel safe here, with you." She teased one hand through the hair on his chest. "Tell me about your family."

It had been years since he'd seen them, but memories still came easily enough. "There were a lot of us. That can happen, when both partners are wolves. I was one of the oldest, but my ma was still having babies when I was damn near thirty."

She bit her lip. "I saw a picture in your box of things. I was... I suppose I was snooping."

He found himself oddly pleased that she'd been interested enough to snoop. "The one of all of us together? Ma had the second set of twins after that was taken, but that was the lot of us, otherwise. More hands to work, but more mouths to feed when things went bad."

"The crops. I remember."

"I was already gone. I'd been gone a couple decades." Considering what she knew of his bootlegging days, it shouldn't have been so hard to admit the truth. But smuggling liquor was a far cry from murder. "I'd had trouble with the law."

She must have felt his tension, because she made a soft noise and rubbed her cheek over his skin. "You don't have to tell me."

He didn't, but it might explain some things. "There are some sweet-talking wizards too. Local preacher was one. We mostly left him alone, until I found out he'd sweet-talked my baby sister into all manner of unnatural things."

She slid her arm around him suddenly and hugged him tight. "What did you do?"

"Shot him. Three times." In broad daylight, because rage had wiggled its way under his skin so fast and hard he couldn't choke it back. "She was barely more than a kid, and he'd twisted her up with dark magic. Took ten years before she'd venture outside without one of our brothers at her side."

"That's horrible," she whispered. "I'm sorry."

He held her closer, because the press of her skin made it easier to deal with the unpleasant memories. "My family hid me. Got me out under the nose of the law. They didn't turn their backs on me until later."

"Until you started working with Seamus?"

"That's the way I was raised. Killing to protect your pack—that's justice. Breaking human laws for money is evil."

She touched his face, her fingers trailing over his stubbled jaw. "Even if it's a stupid human law, I suppose."

He summoned a smile for her. "My mother's thoughts on liquor fall more in line with Joan's than mine."

Simone clucked her tongue. "Liquor doesn't give men the capacity for evil. It doesn't have to."

A fact his mother should have known—but he supposed everyone had prejudices. Even werewolves. "Ain't that the truth. Maybe I'll bring you out there sometime and let you set her straight."

She laughed and punched him lightly in the shoulder. "Don't tease."

He hadn't been. It was so easy to imagine a time after life on the island had settled, when he could bring her ashore and take her to the plains. Easy—and dangerous. For all he knew, she still wanted to go to Europe in the spring.

He'd ask her, if he wasn't so much of a damn coward.

She hummed softly and climbed over him, touching her tongue to his chest and then his shoulder. "I'm not the sort of woman you take home to your family."

It was so contrary to the path of his own thoughts that it shocked him into a laugh. "Oh, honey, you're the sort of woman I'd take anywhere you damn well pleased."

"Really?"

"Truly." And because it hurt to think such a promise could surprise her, he dragged her down into a long, languid kiss, determined to banish conversation with the sweet pleasure of making love to her.

On the tenth night, Simone dreamed of James.

He stood across a wide, dark chasm, calling her name, and her first instinct was to hide. She wasn't ready to face him or anyone else on Breckenridge Island, not when she still had so much to say...

The world spun, shaking beneath her feet, and she almost fell. Strong, sure hands closed around her shoulders, holding her up, but it wasn't Victor.

"James."

"*Finally.*" His voice echoed around them as he dragged her close. "I worried you were dead."

"No, I—" It wasn't a guilty dream at all. *Magic,* she thought fuzzily. "I'm fine. I'm all right."

"I couldn't reach you, but I'm not good at this. I'm not a dream—" His voice faded, though his lips continued to move. A second later sound returned. "—where you are?"

She should have asked Victor to draw a map of some sort to show her, or at least explain it to her. "I don't know. We had to sail off course because of the storm."

His fingers tightened on her shoulders, heat radiating through her clothes to her skin. "You're on one of the islands?"

He shouldn't have been touching her, but she didn't know how to tell him, or even if she should. "An island, yes. There are two summer cabins and a boathouse, if Guy recognizes that."

"How large is it?"

She'd run it from end to end, but always distracted by the call of the waning moon or the thrill of the hunt. The thrill of being chased by her mate. "I don't know. Smaller than Breckenridge, but larger than others."

"I can't—" His body faded, though the heat of his hands on her shoulders burned now. He came back stronger. "I can follow the magic back. I'll come with Guy, we'll find you. I promise we'll find you."

"Even if you can't, we'll be fine. Tell Joan, and Seamus."

"I will. You can—"

He vanished, leaving only the ghostly burn of phantom hands.

She jerked awake, panting, her bare skin so painfully warm she expected to see blisters, or at the very least an angry red imprint of James's fingers.

Instead she found Victor, half sitting up and one hand extended as if to touch her. "Simone?"

It took her a moment to speak. "They found us. James came to me."

"I know." The words were edged with darkness, rough and unsteady. "I can feel him."

James had marked her with magic, the kind that would grate against Victor's instincts under normal circumstances, without his personal experiences complicating the situation. "He did it so they could find us."

His fingers touched her shoulder, and he hissed out a breath. "It's twisted all around you. Is it hurting you?"

She shook her head. "No, it's— They'll find the island. They'll come here."

He snatched his hand away and rolled onto his back, glaring up at the ceiling. "I shouldn't hate it. But I do."

"Victor." She caught herself before reaching for him. "It's a means to an end, that's all. I still—" Her voice broke. "I still belong to you."

In a flash he was stretched out over her, pressing her back against the bed. "Say it again."

Need had tightened his voice, and Simone fed that need readily. Eagerly. "I belong to you. Always, remember?"

Victor pulled back and gripped her hips, urging her over to her stomach with a rough growl. "Again," he whispered, a moment before his teeth closed on her shoulder.

The caress filled her with instinctive satisfaction, the purest sense of belonging tangled up with the desire of a woman for a man. "Yours."

"Mine." Agreement. Confirmation. His fingers tickled

against her skin as he gathered her hair, twisting it around his hand until her nape was bare.

Then he bit her again.

She tried to say his name, but her voice failed, turning the sound into a low, helpless moan.

"Do you want this?" He sat back and stroked his hands down her back until they curved around the flare of her hips. "Do you need it?"

"*You*, Victor." She pushed her hands against mattress, arching her body back toward his. "With every breath."

This wasn't the man who had seduced her with single-minded intensity over long nights. That man had never lost control, not even with instinct driving him. Now, his control seemed to shatter as he urged her hips up, then slid one hand between her thighs. "Prove it. Let me feel it."

She trembled but managed to stay on her knees. His touch stoked a fire in her, one that stole her breath and threatened to shake her apart already. "I'd give you anything."

"Anything?" He slicked his fingers against her, then inside, thrusting deep, using everything he'd learned of her body.

Pleasure built quickly as he coaxed her toward orgasm. Her head began to spin, and she clutched at the blankets until they tore. Her voice rose, hoarse pleas that she barely recognized as her own because nothing mattered, nothing beyond the way he fucked her with his fingers.

He pushed her harder, pushed her until she came, shrieking his name, then thrust home while she still trembled. His hands hit the bed on either side of hers, his chest hot against her back, his breath against her ear. "I can feel you, clenching around my cock. Coming for me."

Simone gasped and shuddered, alight not only with lingering pleasure but with contentment at the yearning in his voice. "It's so much better than anything else, knowing how you want me."

"Under me." He caught her hands and pinned them to the bed before rocking into her again. "Around me. Screaming for me."

She was helpless to escape, completely at his mercy. It should have scared her. Instead, it catapulted her beyond thought.

Beyond sanity.

She turned her head, growled and bit his jaw. "Harder. *Make* me scream."

Teeth closed on her shoulder. Her neck. He marked her again and again, growling each time, thrusting deeper until his hips inched hers up the bed with every powerful movement.

This was claiming, and she never wanted it to end. But nothing could hold release at bay, not with the way Victor moved, every thrust rubbing his cock against a perfect spot inside her.

She came again, screaming this time, and he followed her with a satisfied snarl, driving her hips down to the bed with the force of his final thrust. His head dropped against her shoulder, his body trembling over hers, and one word fell from his lips, low and rasping. "Simone."

She touched his hair, curved her palm to his cheek. *My love.* Would he believe her? And would it matter if he didn't?

After a quiet moment he eased to the side and collapsed, his arm still slung across her back. "Are you all right?"

"Mmm." She could barely move, but she opened her eyes and smiled at him. "Never more right."

He didn't smile back, not right away. His eyes held shadows, an uncertainty. "I wasn't as gentle with you as I'd have liked to be."

The notion that he could have hurt her was so absurd she almost laughed. But he seemed deadly serious, so she chose her words carefully. "You don't always have to be perfectly gentle with me. You couldn't break me unless you tried, and you would never do that."

"I have to be careful. I have to be in *control.*"

"Victor..." She turned to him. "You didn't lose control."

His fingers brushed over her neck, presumably where the mark of his teeth lingered. "Didn't I?"

Simone caught his hand. "You didn't hurt me."

"This time."

"No." She framed his face with her hands and forced him to look at her. "The guilt has to stop, or you're going to make me feel very bad about something that was beautiful."

He closed his eyes and nodded once. "No guilt. It was—" He had to clear his throat. "You're beautiful, Simone. You always are. You're everything."

Her hands trembled. "Then why do I feel like I did something wrong?"

"Shh." His stiff posture broke, and he slid his arms around her and gathered her close. "Sorry, sweetheart. Shouldn't be taking my problems out on you."

"Yes, you should," she argued. "I don't want to be coddled. I want to understand."

"You've been hurt, Simone. You've been mistreated. The fact that you're all right doesn't excuse me losing control to begin with. Strong wolves don't have the luxury of indulging our whims carelessly, no matter how satisfying it can be."

"So you're never allowed to let go, not even with me?"

"Not this soon. Not for the wrong reasons."

It was too pat, too neat, but she had no choice but to

accept his explanation. The alternative was to press him into an argument, and that would only end in tears—or worse.

So she yielded, just like always. "All right."

He wasn't stupid. He knew she wasn't content, she saw the truth of it in his eyes. But whatever haunted him must have been worse, because he pulled her closer and settled the blankets over them. "We need sleep, then. I suppose Guy could be showing up any day now."

Simone closed her eyes, but she couldn't relax into his embrace. He reminded her of the pond at her parents' home in Massachusetts. On the surface, it looked placid, still, and it always iced quickly in the winter. But it was fed by a spring, with currents down in its depths, and that layer of ice remained fragile well into the season.

Victor didn't want her to see what lay below the surface of his emotions. She'd give him time—it was no less than anyone deserved—but, sooner or later, the ice would break.

Chapter Eight

It was wrong to regret being rescued.

Victor stood at the water's edge and watched Guy toss an anchor overboard. The boat floated a good ten yards out into the water, as close as Guy probably wanted to come without knowing what lay under the surface.

A smart move, with Victor standing next to the gutted remains of his sailboat.

Guy waved both arms, but he wasn't the one who jumped right into the chilly water and began swimming.

It was the wizard.

Victor had soothed Simone because it wasn't fair to force her to carry the burden of his own inner darkness, but that darkness stirred as he watched his rival cut a path toward the shore while Guy still struggled with the anchor.

No. Not a rival. His human half.

Hunt, replied the wolf.

He heard Simone coming down the path, heard the moment her steps halted in shock. "Victor."

"I was just about to come get you." Amazing how calm his voice sounded. A faint splash told him Guy had hit the water, probably worried about his wizard friend and the reception he was likely to meet at Victor's hands. Guy *should* be worried, even if Victor managed to keep his tone casual. "I hadn't considered the problem of not having a decent dock. We're going to have to come back later to fetch the supplies."

"I..." Her voice trailed off. "They should be secure in the cabin."

She sounded dazed, and that angry part of himself was all too ready to lay the blame on the wizard now standing shoulder-deep in the surf. He'd wrapped magic around her. Weakened her.

Or maybe she was pleased to see him.

Or maybe you're a bastard who's losing his mind.

Her hand slid into his. "Will we be able to get everything back to Breckenridge before the winter worsens?"

The touch grounded him enough to reply. "I'll talk to Seamus, and we'll send some of the men back. They can make quick work of it."

James struggled onto the rough shore, panting but steadier than Guy, probably owing to who-knew-what sort of magic. Even his voice grated on Victor's nerves. "Simone, thank God! I didn't know if we'd be able to find you, after all."

He reached for her, and she held up a hand even as she stepped back. "James, don't."

It was too late. Victor's temper snapped. His hand closed around the back of James's vest and hauled him back so hard he spilled into the water.

He emerged with Guy's help, sputtering and dripping. "What the hell?"

"*Don't touch her.*"

"Victor, stop." Simone clutched his arm.

James froze in the midst of brushing back his wet hair and stared at Victor. "You bastard."

Even knowing the words were true didn't provide adequate leash to his rage. He crowded Simone back a couple steps and fought to breathe, to *think*. A touch shouldn't unhinge him to the point of violence.

Or maybe it should. He'd never been in love before.

Guy spoke to James, drowning out the wizard's low, angry tones. Simone raised her voice over all of it as she gripped Victor's arms and turned him, her shoulders set and tense. "This is completely unnecessary. It's silly."

It was only in that moment that Victor realized the depths of foolishness his own cowardice had driven him to. In refusing to talk to her, by avoiding the final confrontation that would make her his, he'd left himself unsettled. Wounded.

Everything was about to change, and he didn't know if she'd choose him.

One thing he did know—she wouldn't much care for him if he beat a defenseless man into the ground. "I'm fine," he grated out and prayed it wasn't a lie. "I'm under control now."

"Are you?" She lowered her voice. "Be sure, because we both have to get in a boat with him soon."

"A dunk in the Penobscot Bay will cool my temper plenty."

Simone grasped his face with both hands and studied him intently. Finally, she said, "You still have no idea how I feel about you, do you? None."

His chest hurt. "We can talk about it later. When you're back on Breckenridge Island. Safe."

This time, he wasn't sure she'd give in. But she did—finally, silently—as she folded her arms around her midsection and turned away.

She might as well have slapped him. It would have hurt less.

He would have deserved it more.

Rose shoved another steaming tin cup of broth into her hands. Under Joan's watchful eye, Simone had no choice but to take it. "I'm not cold anymore, really."

"You took a swim in the Atlantic. In November." Joan braced both hands on her hips, her stern expression not nearly strong enough to counteract the worry in her eyes. "James is getting the same treatment."

He'd need it even more. He had magic to protect him, but he'd made the swim twice, to and from the tiny island where she and Victor had been marooned.

Just thinking Victor's name elicited a stab of pain, and Simone closed her eyes. "And Guy? Surely he needs more care, if he's been sailing all over creation, searching for us."

Joan made an amused little noise. "Guy's tucked up with a pot of Rose's best stew and probably has more attention than he wants or needs."

Guilt assailed Simone anew. In her darker moments, she almost resented the tenacity of Guy's rescue efforts. It was, by far, the most selfish and horrible thought she'd ever had. "Has it been terrible without the supplies?"

"We made do." A chair scraped next to her, and Joan sat with a soft sigh. "Necessity is the mother of invention, as they say."

Simone would never be able to look her friend in the eye again if she didn't tell the truth. "I half-hoped we'd have to stay there," she whispered. "With just the two of us, it was..."

Joan's arms came around her. Warm. Strong. "With just the two of you, there was no hiding."

"No, there wasn't." And if he hadn't been forced into such close company with her, things might never have changed. "I

215

can't go back to having him ignore me because he doesn't know what else to do, Joanie. I won't make it."

"I know." Sympathy stood clearly in Joan's eyes, and a more subtle warmth surrounded them both, the comfort of pack. "Don't let him. Dominant wolf or not, he's still a man. And men are cowards. Stand up to him and make him deal with you. It's better than not knowing, isn't it?"

"It's not *me* he has to deal with. It's more complicated, and I have no idea how to help him."

"Do you think it's a man thing or a wolf thing? Because I don't understand men, but I understand strong wolves."

Victor's past hurts were dark and far too personal for her to share with Joan. "It's both."

"Well, then." Joan pulled back and crossed her arms over her chest. "It pains me to give Victor this much credit, but it *is* the truth. He can't choose whether or not he wants to protect you. None of us can. We could cut out our own hearts trying to stop and we'd still fail."

"I know." That instinct had driven Victor to rage before, to kill. "I need to talk to him."

"When you've rested." Joan stood and tucked the chair back under the table. "Rose will stay with you. I'm going to make sure everything's settled and see who can be organized to retrieve the supplies."

"Thanks." As her friend began to turn away, Simone stopped her with a hand on her arm. "You and Victor don't give each other enough credit, Joan. You're more alike than you think."

"No, we know exactly how alike we are." Joan glanced over her shoulder, one eyebrow raised. "Or have you never noticed how little credit we give ourselves?"

"Perhaps I have." Nothing would make either of them more

uncomfortable than peering into a mirror—and not liking what they saw.

Joan nodded in silent acknowledgement before slipping on her coat and bundling out into the crisp evening wind.

Rose remained at the stove, as if she hadn't heard a bit of the conversation. For all Simone knew, she hadn't. "Thank you for cooking, Rose."

"I don't mind." The younger woman turned and wiped her hands on the thick, rough apron tied over her slacks and sweater. "I missed you. We all did. We were so worried, Simone."

She smiled over the rim of her cup. "But you managed, right?"

"We managed." Rose poured herself a mug of tea and took Joan's abandoned chair. "The men were...surprisingly comforting. I wasn't sure how they'd be without Victor here to glare at them for flirting."

How much of Victor's glaring had been due to his own harsh judgment of himself? "I assume they behaved."

"For the most part. There was a bit of a scandal with Mary and Thomas, but... Well, you know Mary. And Seamus took care of it quick enough."

Simone's smile faded a little, though she tried to keep it in place. "Sounds like you all got along just fine without us."

Rose's eyebrows drew together. "We managed," she repeated, a little more forcefully this time. "If you think we weren't missing you every day, you're mad."

"No, I—" She set her cup on the table and propped both elbows beside it. "I had a lot of time to think."

"About what?"

She took a deep breath. "I wouldn't blame you, any of you, if you hated me."

Incomprehension filled Rose's face. She opened her mouth. Closed it. Frowned. "I...I don't understand."

Oh, how well she had hidden herself. "For not protecting you from Edwin. For not stopping him."

Rose's confusion didn't vanish. If anything, it became more acute. For an endless moment she stared at Simone, the silence growing more and more uncomfortable as understanding blossomed in the girl's eyes, followed swiftly by anger. "And how many of us do you hold accountable with you? Should we all shoulder the guilt for every girl who came after us, even though we were surviving as best we could?"

"It isn't the same." Simone's misery deepened. "I keep wondering if I could have found a way, back before he went truly mad."

"I'm familiar with his madness," Rose said stiffly. "And I don't think it was madness at all. He was a man who could indulge every whim because his money gave him power. How would you have stopped that? Joan is the strongest of us all, and even she couldn't stop him on her own."

Reasonable words, with a reasonable point. "I don't know, Rose. I can't help feeling I should have *found* a way."

"I know. Perhaps you could have. Or perhaps you would have died, and Joan would have had no one to give *her* strength while she fought to protect us." Rose's anger faded a little. "For some of us, the worst Edwin could do was still better than what we would have had. You and Joan lost so much to Edwin. I didn't have anything for him to take."

"I'm sorry." Her guilt was selfish, borne of blindness. To many of Edwin's conquests, the abuse they suffered at his hands was a mere extension of their lives before, just more of the same. At least at his mansion, they'd also had a warm, dry place to sleep and plenty to eat. "I'm sorry."

Rose smiled and shook her head. "Don't be sorry. You still

don't understand. You think we deserved better. You made me believe I deserved better. The life we have now...I know it's not much to you and Joan, but for me, it's a dream."

A dream, one Simone could help realize and build—but only if she stayed. She wiped her eyes and blew out a shaky breath. "I got you a new book in Searsport. Fairy tales."

Rose's smile lost its melancholy edge. "I love fairy tales. Thank you."

Because she hadn't experienced nearly enough of them. "You're welcome."

Rose leaned in to rest her cheek against Simone's blanketed shoulder. "We got by without you, but only because you taught us how to do it. How to be strong enough."

It was the sort of comfort she'd dispensed a thousand times, and she'd never needed it herself more than she did at that moment.

Between the thrill of knowing Simone was safe and the agony of wondering if he'd lost her completely, Victor had forgotten one very important detail.

He no longer had a place to sleep.

Nightfall found him cradling a mug of coffee he'd brewed over the hearth in the common building, a blanket thrown over his shoulders in a pointless attempt to protect against the chill. It couldn't protect against the icy misery of loneliness.

He was a fool.

Seamus put it more bluntly. "You're a blooming asshole, Vic."

The alpha didn't ask if he could sit. Why would he? A bench scraped across the rough floor, and Victor glared over at the man who'd gotten him into this mess to begin with. "Maybe I'm not cut out for life on an island."

"It can be confining," Seamus agreed, holding out a shiny silver insulated bottle. "Rose sent you some hot soup. Thought you might need it."

Popping the lid filled the room with the scent of rich broth and herbs. It would no doubt be delicious—the girl could cook so well the men would already be circling if she weren't so clearly wary—but Victor would have traded it in a heartbeat to be back in that cabin, laughing over Simone's slightly burned bunny stew.

Christ, he *was* an asshole. "I don't trust myself with her."

"Why?"

"I would have ripped the wizard's arms off for touching her."

Seamus snorted. "He wants her for his own. The urge is understandable."

To men who'd been wolves for decades, perhaps. "Not to Simone."

"Mmm." His friend nodded slowly. "So she thinks you doubt her."

Victor frowned. That possibility hadn't even occurred to him. That she was scared of him was easy to believe. That she felt wary of the violence inside, the violence that led him to lash out. What woman wouldn't be, especially when she'd been so poorly treated?

Seamus leaned forward. "Quit gaping at me and tell me what she did when you tried to pummel James."

He struggled to remember. "Tried to get me to stop, I guess."

"And do you think she did that for *his* benefit, or for yours?"

No, he wasn't an asshole *or* a fool. He was an idiot. A self-absorbed one. "Fine, I get it."

Seamus waved away his words. "Do you? You look at the wizard and you see a rival. Of course you do. But maybe Simone doesn't understand that, because maybe he can't compete with you at all."

"I said *I get it.*" It came out as more of a snarl than he'd usually level at his alpha, but having his nose shoved into the truth like an errant puppy was less comfortable than taking a midwinter swim in the Penobscot Bay. "Leave off, Seamus. Or have you decided to give up being alpha in favor of matchmaking, after all?"

Seamus ground his teeth audibly as he rose. "The attitude has to go, Vic. You want me to mind my own fucking business, I will. But the woman in question is Joan's best friend, and if you break her heart because you're too proud to fix your problems, I'll beat your ass."

Less than two weeks on that island, and he'd already grown accustomed to being the alpha of a pack of two. Seamus wouldn't hesitate to kick him back into line if necessary, even if a challenge would damage the feeling of safety they'd fought so hard to cultivate.

So Victor lowered his eyes. Not for long, just enough to acknowledge that his fight wasn't with his alpha. "I understand."

"Uh-uh, this isn't your alpha talking. This is *me*, your friend, telling you that you can hate me for interfering if you want, but don't fuck this up."

Victor squared his shoulders and looked up. "I'll try."

"Then I'll leave you alone." He gestured to the bottle. "If you want more, Rose stashed it in the big kitchen. Last I heard, she was tending to Simone."

Food wouldn't hurt. It would settle his stomach and give him time to think. To steel his nerves for what he had to do next. "Where's James?"

"At home. He's well-equipped to handle his own recovery."

James was the one of the few on the island who had his own home, but since more than half of it was given over to the infirmary and his medical supplies, no one begrudged him the privacy. At least it would make the coming confrontation easier.

Only Simone could make it worth it.

James answered his door on the fifth knock, with a good-sized glass of Scotch in one hand. "To what do I owe this honor?"

"Can I come in?"

The blond man stepped back with a sweeping gesture. "Be my guest, Mr. Bowen."

Not the most promising start, but Victor stepped inside and turned to face James. "I shouldn't have lost control. I'm sorry."

"You're not sorry," James countered politely. "You're full of shit."

Victor shrugged. "I *am* sorry I lost control. For her sake, if nothing else. I'm sure as hell not here for my ego."

"Then why are you here?" He dropped his drink on the table with a thump. "So I can absolve you of your guilt?"

"Because Simone told me where you're going in the spring."

For the first time, some of the man's tension faded, but he retrieved his drink, as if he hadn't meant to put it down at all. "If you're worried I might still press her to accompany me, relax. I withdraw my invitation."

A selfish part of him rejoiced. No danger from a greater purpose, no choices for Simone. She'd be trapped on the island, his only rival a continent away. She'd be his.

But not really. "That's not what I want," Victor said, and if it was a lie, at least the wizard would never know. "I want to know if you'd only bring her if she was your lover."

"I told Simone her participation was in no way contingent upon her being in my bed," James said, "and I meant it."

No turning back. "And if she's in my bed? Would you let me come with you?"

The man almost choked on his liquor. "*You* want to go to Europe to fight for peace?"

"No. But she does, and I'll fight for her. For any damn thing she wants."

Judging by the wizard's expression, the words had been unexpected. "Honestly, I'm not sure what to say." He finished his drink, then shrugged. "If you both want to help out, you're both welcome. There are so few people willing to even take a chance at peace that my uncle can probably find tasks for anyone willing to try. It might not be glamorous work, though."

It made James a better man than him, and Victor might admit it out loud. Someday. For now... "We'll have the winter to discuss it."

He snorted out a laugh. "Perhaps by spring I won't even mind so much. We'll see, yes?"

"We'll see." Their truce felt fragile enough that Victor backed toward the door, past ready to be gone. "Thanks for finding us."

"You're welcome." James sighed roughly. "Don't hurt her. She deserves to be happy."

"I know." The only question was if he was ready to deserve being happy with her.

Chapter Nine

Simone frowned and watched Rose gather the last of her things. "You really don't have to go."

Rose smiled and folded her extra blanket with a little too much attention to how all of the corners matched up. "Nonsense. You deserve one night of peace before you have to deal with all of us again."

"But surely you shouldn't have to *leave* for the night."

"It's just one night." She was still fiddling with the blanket, smoothing down the creases. The other two girls who shared their tiny one-room house had already left, both expressing a sudden interest in squeezing in with friends for the evening.

Simone's desperation grew. If they left her alone, she'd have nothing to distract her from thoughts of—

She groaned. "Seamus put you up to this, didn't he?" Victor was probably already on his way over.

Rose looked up and wrinkled her nose. "He's the alpha. We obey. And Joan—" Her lips curved up in a tiny smile. "Well. Joan said she'd be along in an hour or so anyway, to make sure you weren't alone tonight unless you wanted to be. *She* doesn't obey."

"No, she doesn't." Joan would never have given in to Victor the way she had, allowed him to hide so that things deteriorated to such a sad state. "Was Seamus so sure Victor would come tonight?"

"Sure enough to give up his wife's company for the evening if Victor doesn't." The girl pulled on her warm knit cap and picked up her bundle of blankets and clothing. "If you need anything, if you need me—I'll just be a few steps down the path. I'll come back, I promise, no matter what the alpha says or thinks."

Simone's hands had started to shake, and she tucked them into her pockets. "Either way, I'll be fine. Tomorrow, after breakfast, though. Our next lesson exchange."

"Fairy tales," Rose agreed, striding toward the door. She paused with her hand on the cool metal knob. "I hope you get yours."

She already had, for a while. "I will, if I have anything to say about it."

A heavy knock rattled the door hard enough to drive a startled yelp out of Rose. Color filled her cheeks as she slapped her free hand over her mouth. "Maybe Joan ran out of patience."

But Simone already knew who stood on the other side. "Have a good night, Rose. I'll see you in the morning."

Rose pulled open the door and dropped her gaze, inching aside to let Victor pass. He stepped across the threshold, then bent low enough to catch Rose's eyes. "Thank you for the soup."

She nodded with a small, shy smile. "Have a good night, Mr. Bowen. Simone."

She practically ran away, and Simone steeled herself against the way her body reacted to Victor's presence. It was the same as always, a hunger that went straight to her bones, only so much sharper now that—

Now that he's been yours.

Simone squared her shoulders. "Come in, Victor."

225

Victor closed the door quietly behind him and turned to lean against it. "Simone."

"How are you feeling?"

"Well enough. Rose sent me soup."

"Good." He was nervous, *she* was nervous, and the whole thing was just ridiculous. "This is insane. Why are we tiptoeing around one another like strangers?"

His lips tugged up in that half smile she'd come to know so well. "Because it seems like we just woke up."

"Maybe we did." *Now or never, Simone.* She took a step forward. "I have some things to say, things I've held inside far too long."

The smile faded. "I'm listening."

She took a deep breath. "I told you once that, if you needed time, I would wait for you. Well, it's still true. I love you, and that's not going to change, so I'll wait. One of these days, you won't have any choice but to believe me."

After a moment, Victor nodded. "I may need time. Not to love you. Not even to believe in you. I need time to learn how to be what you need."

"What do you think I need?"

He didn't answer. Not quite. "I talked to James before I came here."

There were only a handful of things the two of them would have ever discussed, even under the best of circumstances. "About the trip overseas this spring."

Another nod. "I asked if I could go."

He couldn't have. Victor was the last person who should have wanted to end the war between werewolves and wizards. He should have wanted to *fight*. "You'd go...for me?"

He might claim not to have an affinity for words, but he

made the ones he used count. "I'd do anything for you."

It stole her breath, because it wasn't a grand declaration, just a simple statement of fact. Her eyes welled with tears as she tried to answer, but the only sound that emerged was a strangled sob.

"Oh, Christ." In two seconds he was at her side, both arms sliding around her. "This is why I don't talk. All I ever do is say the wrong thing."

"Don't be daft." She barely had time to breathe the words before her mouth landed on his in a quick, desperate kiss. "If you say what's in your heart, it'll always be right."

Victor lifted a hand to her hair, smoothing it back before sinking his fingers into the bulk of it. "Then why in hell are you crying, woman?"

"Because you have no idea how wonderful you are."

He smiled, a real smile that lit up his eyes. "Don't waste tears over that. You've got all the time in the world to teach me."

It would take a long time to heal the scars that plagued him, no matter what, but it would never happen if he couldn't open up to her. "Will you be honest with me, Victor? Will you help me understand you?"

"I'll be honest. Starting now." Strong hands coaxed her head back. "I love you. And I want to protect you from everything. Even things you don't need protecting from. Even from myself. You have to understand that I mean well, and kick me into line when meaning well isn't enough."

"I can do that." She didn't have to worry about driving him away with her demands. "And we don't have to go to Europe with James. All I need is to be useful, to *do* something. All other things being equal, I'd just as soon do that here."

If he was relieved, he didn't show it. Instead he pressed a gentle kiss to her forehead. "No need to decide right off. We have a whole winter ahead of us, and in the spring... Well, before we go anywhere else, I was hoping you might take a different sort of trip with me."

Only one thing could be that important to him. "Your family?"

"Mmm. It might be time. I've turned over a new leaf."

"Decided to settle down into that quiet life."

He leaned over until his lips brushed hers, soft and warm. "Found a reason. And a woman I want to bring home to my mother."

The temptation to fall into the kiss almost overwhelmed her. "There's one more thing, Victor. It's important."

"Tell me."

"You scared yourself the other night, when I had that dream." Even with all the promises, it was surprisingly hard to form the words. "Tell me you won't always have to hold back with me."

He didn't answer at once. Instead he studied her face, giving the request serious consideration. When he finally answered, his words held the strength of truth. "We both need to learn our boundaries, and that won't happen overnight. But it won't last forever, either."

It might have been easier for him to lie to please her, but he didn't. "Then we take our time."

"We do." He kissed her jaw, then her ear, his breath warm against her skin. "And I've already learned some of your boundaries. I won't hold back from them again."

No power could have kept her from kissing him then, from slipping her arms around his neck and holding him close, with nothing held back. No reason to hide. "I love you."

This time, he didn't run. "I love you too, gorgeous."

She started to ask him to stay the night, then cursed softly as she remembered his ruined boat—and home. "Where are you going to sleep now?"

"I'll find a place. Or maybe *we* can find a place. May not be quite as much privacy as my boat..." He lifted a hand and smoothed his thumb over her cheek. "We can still sneak away."

"We can buy another boat come spring." She turned her head and nipped at his thumb.

Victor backed her toward the bed, a wicked gleam in his eyes. "Mmm. Which means tonight might be our last uninterrupted night of privacy."

"I refuse to even entertain the possibility," she murmured, a heavy anticipation warming her. "Like you said, we can sneak away."

"And we will." He kissed her cheek. "Every chance we get." Another warm kiss, this time to her jaw. "But tonight..." His teeth closed on her throat, gentle but firm, and magic curled around her. "Tonight you're all mine."

"I told you already, I belong to you." An easy promise to make, now that she knew the truth. They would struggle from time to time, with themselves and with each other, but nothing would ever bring them as much happiness as making that effort and staying together. It wasn't the fairy tale Rose had wished for her, but something better. Something real. Something that wouldn't end just because dawn had broken and real life had overtaken dreams.

Always.

About the Author

How do you make a Moira Rogers? Take a former forensic science and nursing student obsessed with paranormal romance and add a computer programmer with a passion for gritty urban fantasy. To learn more about this romance-writing, crime-fighting duo, visit their webpage at www.moirarogers.com, or drop them an email at moira@moirarogers.com. (Disclaimer: crime-fighting abilities may appear only in the aforementioned fevered imaginations.)

These elements have no desire to be tamed...

Stormchild
© *2010 Vivian Arend*
Pacific Passion, Book 1

As the new traveling doctor for the Pacific Inside Passage settlements, Matthew Jentry balances dual roles for his water-shifter people—caring for their health as a human-trained physician, and for their spiritual needs as a shaman.

Distractions of the female kind are not on his agenda, but his magical bloodline makes him a target for every marriage-minded woman within range. There's something about the mysterious Laurin Marshall, though, that he finds far too enticing. It's just as well that it's time for him to move on.

Laurin thought she had perfected her guise as a mild-mannered teacher, but the sexual fireworks she and Matt touch off are threatening to blow her cover out of the water. Luckily it's time for her to catch the boat to her next assignment.

When she discovers she'll be sailing with Matt, she realizes there's only one thing more dangerous than their unforgettable one-night stand—being trapped with him on a boat that gives "riding out the storm" a whole new meaning...

Warning: Contains strong sexual currents and powerful waves of desire that break down inhibitions. Recommended only for those able to navigate through extremely steamy situations, on land and at sea.

CPSIA information can be obtained at www.ICGtesting.com
Printed in the USA
243129LV00001BA/174/P